The Protectors

The Protectors

LARRY WADE LIVINGSTON

Library of Congress Control Number:		2019916048
ISBN:	Hardcover	978-1-7960-6512-1
	Softcover	978-1-7960-6511-4
	eBook	978-1-7960-6510-7

Print information available on the last page.

Rev. date: 10/09/2019

To order additional copies of this book, contact:
Xlibris
1-888-795-4274
www.Xlibris.com
Orders@Xlibris.com
803931

Contents

Characters ix

Kodiac Island, Alaska 5

Puerto Villamil, Galapagos Island Chain 9

Institute for Oceanography 11

The Deceptive 14

Puerto Villamil 16

The Cell 19

Institute for Oceanoghaphy 23

Sydney Australia 24

The Secret World Below 27

Hawaii 31

Atlanta 33

The Cell 37

Puerto Villamil 38

Alaska, Kodiac Island 40

Puerto Villamil, Galapagos 42

The Cell 44

The Secret World Below 46

Ecuador 48

Alaska 50

Australia 52

Atlanta CDC 55

Washington DC...56

Institute of Oceanoghaphy 57

Washington D C 59

The Secreat World Below 61

The CDC...65

Alaska, Kodiak Island 67

The Cell..69

CDC..70

The Deceptive...75

Australia...76

Washington DC...79

Institute of Oceanograph..81

History of the Secreat Worlds Habitants.........................84

The CDC...89

The Goracks 93

The Cell..96

The Goracks 98

The Cell..100

The Goracks 101

The CDC...103

Klamath Falls, Oregon 105

Washington D C 111

Institute of Oceanography 114

Klamath Falls, Oregon 119

Hawaii 122

The Hope...129

The Goracks 131

The Hope 138

The Deceptive 139

Klamath Falls, Oregon 141

The Galapagos Islands 143

The Hope 145

The Goracks 147

The Hope 154

Klamath Falls 157

Klamath Falls, Oregon 168

Hawaii, The Hope 175

Washington D C 176

Klamath Falls, Oregon 178

Washington D C 180

Washington D C 184

The Hope 185

Klamath Falls, Oregon 188

CDC Atlanta 192

The Cell 193

The Goracks 195

Washington D C 196

Institute of Oceanograph 198

Klamath Falls, Oregon 201

CDC Atlanta 204

Klamath Falls, Oregon 206

Author's Perspective 209

CHARACTERS

CAPTAIN	TROY BOMBER	1
FIRST MATE	STEVE MILKEN	2
SONAR TECH	BOBBY GRAY	3
HEAD ENGINEER	MATT STRONG	4
DIVER	CARL	5
DIVER	TONY	6
INSTITUTE OF OCEAN	JOHN TYLOR	7
INSTITUTE	ERIC SLOAN	8
INSTITUTE	DAVE CORNELL	9
STATE DEPT	BILL WILSON	10
PRESIDENT	TRAVER BLACK.	11
COAST GUARD	CAPTAIN TOME	12
I O OCEAN ASST.	TIM DAY	13
REPORTER	SAM TALLOW	14
CAMERAMAN	TED WILCOX	15
CAPTAIN RUSSIA	CHEZCOV	16
EDITOR	LEW SKINNER	17
INTERN	MARY RUSH	18
SONAR TECH	BRAD MILLER	19
COM TECH	JIMMY BARNS	20
PALEONTOLOGIST DR. ZURICH	CDC	21

THE CELL	DR. ERICA JONES	22
THE CELL	DR CLAY WANG	23
AUSSI BOATMAN	JOSH HOPPER	24
DEAD MAN-STINGERS	KEVIN TROTTER	25
SYDNEY DOCTOR	DR. HOWARD SHAW	26
MIGRATION PATTERN	DR. THOMAS ELVAN	27
LEADER OF GORACK'S	RODIC	28
FOLLOWER, GORACK	JONG	29
LIMO DRIVER	BRENT SMITH	30
HOSTESS CDC	SARAH WINTERS	31
DOCTOR CDC	JIMMY STONER	32
SEAMAN-COAST GUARD	CHRIS	33
GENETICS/GENES/CDC	DR. LANCE MOTTO	34
RODIC'S WIFE	SAREN	35
RODICS SON	BASEL	36
RODICS DAUGHTER	GOTHY	37
FOLLOWER, GORACK	PAGE	38
PRESIDENTS ASST.	AMY PIRECE	39
DR. CDC	JILL LAMONT	40
DR. CDC	JACK LINTNER	41
F-15 PILOT	CAP, RODNEY BROWN	42
CELL DR.	DR. RIP MOTE	43
REPTILE EXPERT	DR. IGOR BOTANIC	44
PERU	PRESIDENT GARCIA	45
ECUADOR	PRESIDENT SANCHEZ	46
COLUMBIA	PRESIDENT GOMEZ	47
TAXI HAWAII	JOSE RAMARAO	48
SHARK EXPERT	DR. NICK BROWNSTONE	49
HUNTER	BOB	50
HUNTER	JOE	51
GAME WARDEN	VAN GREEN	52
VICE PRESIDENT	RICHARD MOREHOUSE	53

SHERIFF	RICH WATTS	54
INSTITUTE BOSS	BEN SHAW	55
INSTITUTE PHY	JIM WHEELER	56
INSTITUTE NURSE	AMY BAKER	57
POLICE CHIEF	CAP ROY ANDERS	58
MAINTENANCE	BOBBY SMITH	59
F-12 PILOT	CAPTAIN SNOW	60
VOLCANOS	MR. DON MASTERS	61
GALAPAGOS DR.	DR. TRAVOR LITTLE	62
GORACK	BULIA & WIFE	63
GORACK	KIRIT & WIFE	64
GORACK	TRERD	65
K F DEPUTY	OFFICE ALLEN LOOMS	66
SCIENTIST	PROFESSOR KOVICHA	67
ARMY CORP	MJ. THOMAS LEWIS	68
ARMY CORP	KEN TIPLORD	69

"Captain, sonar shows something really big closing in on us from the rear," Bobby Grey the sonar technician said.

"How big and how fast?" Captain Troy Bomber asked.

"It's big and moving at thirty knots plus, right at us Captain."

"Sound the dive alert and dive at the maximum decent speed and see if it follows."

The alarm sounds and the submarine started a rapid decent at an extreme angle. The crew was holding on to anything that would support their weight as they went deeper and deeper.

There was a loud yell as something struck the sub and actually spun it around 180 degrees. The sound of being hit was deafening and caused a major concern if they had water coming in from a ruptured hull.

"Damage control, damage control," screamed the Captain.

"No seeable damage Captain. Engineering room is good and all engines are performing as usual. I will double check everything again Captain, to see if I missed something," said Head Engineer Matt Strong.

"Whatever it was, has gone Captain," said Bobby.

"Surface, blow all tanks. I want to see if there's damage on the outside. Have the dive team suit up. I want them to inspect the propellers for damage and the rudder."

The submarine broke the water and splashed down without incident. The hatch popped open and the Captain and dive team exited the sub. The two divers slipped into the water and the Captain was joined by the Executive Officer in the lookout.

"What the hell was that Captain?" Said XO Steve Milken.

"I have no idea Steve. I'm going to find out no matter how long it takes. We can't have something like this threatening our fleet or any ship for that matter."

The divers returned and gave their damage report to the Captain.

"One propeller is slightly bent, but not enough to alter its function. There is a large dent in the port backside of the submarine. It didn't cause a rupture or hole for water to leak in. It does need to be repaired sooner than later," said the divers.

"Thank you, Seaman for that report. I'm turning the sub around and going back to port for repairs.

XO, call Hawaii and inform them we are on our way back for repairs. Don't expand on what repairs or how the damage occurred. I don't want what happened said over the radio, we need to know what we are dealing with first."

"Yes Captain, right away."

The Deceptive slowly made its way back to the Navy's Pearl Harbor repair dock. It was met by several Admirals and C I A officials. Captain Bomber and XO Milken were immediately taken to a secure location for debriefing and explanation of how they acquired the subs damage.

The meeting lasted for hours. However, it ended with more questions than answers. The Navy had to find out what had attacked their sub. The C I A and the National Security Department needed to know as well.

Had this been a trial run for a future terrorist attack? Was it a new weapon being developed by China, Russia or North Korea? The government looked at every possibility, no matter how bazar. The possibility of a sea monster or extraterrestrial was looked at and quickly removed from the table as not being feasible.

Over the next few weeks as the submarine was being repaired, several reports came in of similar attacks. Most were from the exact area that the Deceptive had received its damage. The strange thing was that the attacks were taking place above the Mariana Trench.

The Deceptive wasn't capable of reaching the bottom of the tremendous depth of the Mariana Trench. (36,100 ft). Captain Bomber had orders to stay in the area and monitor it for any further activity or unexplainable events.

The Navy and the National Security Department both launched investigations into the attack on the Deceptive.

As usual Green Peace and other environmental organizations showed up to literally spy on the governments search for answers. Sometimes you have to wonder if any of them have something better to do. The governments silent feelings on the matter, was that they were a bunch of spoiled rich kids and hadn't worked a day in their life.

Another week passed and then hundreds of people on the beach began screaming and yelling for help. Many took out their smart phones and filmed what was happening.

There were three Great White sharks in the water attacking swimmers and surfers. They would shoot straight out of the water and swallow whomever they had set their sights on.

By the time everyone had exited the water the sharks had eaten 14 people. There were adults and children that were among the deceased. Eleven had been surfing and the other three were children swimming.

It was a horrific sight and an event that still haunts everyone that were present that day. Shark attacks always give concerns about safety. These attacks caused even more than just concern.

As experts watched and evaluated the footage gleaned from the many smart phones they had confiscated: the conclusion was that the three sharks each would measure over fifty feet in length.

Dr. John Tylor, head of the Institute for Oceanography in Honolulu was mesmerized by the data being found. "There's no way this data can be valid. It's impossible for a great White to grow to be 50 feet in length. Eric, did you run these calculations two or three times, or just once?"

"I ran them three times doctor. I couldn't believe the results myself. I even had Dave Cornell double check my figures."

Eric Sloan and Dave Cornell were both 20-year veterans working at the Institute. It was thought that when Dr. Tylor retired one of them would be selected to replace him.

"I've got to notify Washington and see what the suits decide we should do from this point on." Dr. Tylor said.

He called his friend Bill Wilson at the State Department and asked him who would be the right person to contact about the situation. After explaining the details to his friend, Bill decided to hold a conference call.

"Mr. President, Bill Wilson of the State Department. I have the renowned Doctor John Tylor from the Institute for Oceanography on the line. I think you should hear what he has to say Mr. President."

"Fine Bill, if its important enough for you to call, it must be warranted." President Traver Black said."

Dr. Tylor explained his findings and his concerns if his evaluations were correct. The consensus was that if there was something causing this mutation, what else might be being affected?

"I find your data alarming for sure Dr. Tylor. Bill, I'm putting you in charge of seeing that Dr. Tylor get's all the help from the government he needs. Keep me advised to your findings daily and carry out this investigation as quietly as possible.

I will instruct agencies to cooperate with Project Stingray. That's the name of this investigation from here on out." President Black said.

"Thank you, Mr. President. I will get on this matter today. I will turn over my duties at the State Department to assistant Brad Turner in my absence."

"Good Bill, find out what the hell is going on out there in the Pacific. I need to know if we are facing an environmental catastrophe or a foreign plot."

With in an hour, Bill Wilson was on a plane bound for Honolulu. He was worried about what Project Stingray would reveal. He hoped it would turn out that the three sharks were mutations due to massive inbreeding. He was reaching, but any other reason would be horrifying.

KODIAC ISLAND, ALASKA

Over the last two months, several fishing boats had left the harbor, but never returned. At first the locals thought that the Russians were involved in their disappearance. Since there hadn't been any mayday broadcast, that possibility faded.

It wasn't until the 5th boat disappeared that the F B I and Homeland Security were notified by the Alaska government. It was something they wanted to keep quiet so as not to affect tourism. However, the time had come that they really had no other option.

Needless to say, the Washington D C officials were majorly disappointed in their delay of reporting the situation.

There were two places that were having these attacks. The U S Government was aware of that, but neither place knew about the other.

Great Whites aren't usually found swimming in the Bering Sea, Dr. Tylor thought to himself as he boarded a Navy plane for Alaska. He left his associate Tim Day in charge of the Hawaii investigation while he was on vacation. (What Mr. Day was told for him leaving).

Once Dr. Tylor arrived on Kodiak Island, he found a harbor half full of boats. He was met by Captain Tome of the Coast Guard.

"Welcome Dr. Tylor. I'm Captain EricToma and was told to expect your arrival today."

"Thank you, Captain. What's the latest on your situation?"

"As you can see, only half the slips are occupied. Every empty one represents a boat that has vanished. The reason you see the boats that are here now, is because their afraid to go out of the harbor. Until the problem no longer exists, no way will anyone venture out in the Bering Sea again."

"Did Bill Wilson at the State Department contact you about taking me out to tomorrow?"

"Yes, our biggest boat is being fueled and stocked so we can stay out for at least four days. Earlier this morning, several boxes of scientific equipment arrived and it too is being installed right now."

"Great, that's sensitive data recording devices and tracking sonar and charting equipment."

"Follow me and I'll show you to your room at the Hilton Hotel doctor."

Dr. Tylor went to bed early. He knew the next day was going to be the start of a long and tedious week. He wanted to discover the reason for the disappearances as fast as possible. The truth was, he wasn't fond of the cold and preferred the warm breeze of the big island.

The morning came fast and uneventful. Dr. Tylor was pleased that he had gotten 9 hours of noninterrupted sleep. He had been working long hard hours before coming to Alaska. He now was faced with even longer and harder work in the cold and stuck on a boat.

Captain Tome introduced Dr. Tylor to the boats crew. Then they had a hardy breakfast in the boat's galley. With a long blast of the boats horn, they headed out of the harbor and out to sea.

Except for a couple of Russian fishing trawlers, the sea was deserted of any boats. Captain Tome brought his boat up close to one if the Russian ships.

"Captain Chezcov, how's the wife and kids?" Captain Tome asked.

"There fine my friend. How are yours?"

"There okay too. How's the fishing going?"

"Very slow Eric, since the attacks on smaller fishing vessels. My catch weight has suffered as much as 45 percent less and continuing to get worse."

"Sorry to hear that Captain. Have you heard about any new attacks in the last few days?"

"Something rammed my ship yesterday. It was enormous in size on our sonar screen. We never had a visual of it, but it damn near lifted the ship out of the water. It only made that one hard strike and then disappeared into deep water."

"Where did that take place Captain?"

"Ten miles Southeast of Seal Rock, along the drop off ledges of Stutters Fault."

"Thank you, Captain, good fishing. I'm going to go investigated that incident. We need to solve this mystery for everyone's sake."

"I didn't know we were that friendly with the Russians." Dr. Tylor stated.

"Yea, I found it easier to befriend them instead of being confrontational. It's a little jester that goes a long way. We both adhere to the international water laws and regulations. However, we both let little infractions slide by.

I tell him where the fish are if I know. I always recommend an area in his or international waters. Captain Chezcov is a nice guy. His crew and mine exchange gifts, like chocolate bars for Russian Vodka."

"Sounds like a nice arrangement you've worked out"

"Yea, it works, with nobody getting hurt and it reduces the stress level."

It took two hours to reach Stutters Fault. Once there, Dr Tylor set up his equipment with the help of some crew members. Captain Tome supplied three of his men to assist Dr. Tylor monitoring the equipment. The three men were the backups to the ones that held the communication, sonar and navigational positions.

At dinnertime everyone was in the galley playing cards, eating or writing letters to someone. When out of nowhere a huge deafening bang was heard and the boat tilted 45 degrees before splashing back down to its previous level position.

"What the hell was that?" Could be heard echoing throughout the boat.

Captain Tome and Dr. Tylor both rushed to the observation deck. They scanned the water with high range binoculars and with the naked eye. At first, they saw nothing and as time passed, they decided to return to the galley.

As they turned to leave the deck, the boat again was struck and the boat rose at least two feet above the water. It crashed violently back down into the water with such a massive jolt that some of the crew received chipped teeth.

As if by magic, both Dr. Tylor and Captain Toma saw the creature that was responsible for the attack. It was a Killer Whale like no other. This Orca was a minimum 250 feet long and 80 feet wide.

With its mouth open, it could easily swallow the Coast Guard boat they were standing on. It could demolish the boat with a swipe of its tail.

Captain Toma ran to the bridge area and shouted commands. The engines revved up and a course set to return to the harbor.

"There's no reason to stay here Dr. Tylor. You saw what's causing the disappearances. I'm not going to put the lives of my crew in danger at this point. The solution to this problem is way over my pay grade.

There's nothing we can do to control that creature. This is a job for the military and government suits to carry out," Captain Toma said.

Captain Toma called the State Department and explained the situation to them. The State Department relayed the facts to the military and President Black.

The President called an emergency meeting with the heads of each military branch and several heads of the most prestigious think tank organizations. He called in experts from the fields of oceanography, environmental and FEMA readiness response.

PUERTO VILLAMIL, GALAPAGOS ISLAND CHAIN

Reporter Sam Tallow and his cameraman Ted Wilcox stood tall as people ran by them screaming.

"Get that Ted, Get that son-of-a-bitch on film." John demanded.

"Shut the hell up, I know my fricking job."

"Close enough, RUN! I'm not going to be a fricking snack for that thing." John said.

They both turned and ran with the other people to any tall building. Everyone felt safe when they reached the third floor of a structure.

Everyone looked out windows and watched the movements of the Komodo Dragan below as it stalked its way through the town. Relief spread quickly as the lizard disappeared into the forest. The fear remained, but for the moment they could gather their emotions.

"I've never seen something like that Ted. I hope you got every inch of that bastard on film."

"I've got it, I told you already. Besides, for your information it's digital. Not stupid film you idiot. How did you get this job anyway?"

"Show it to me. I want to see it for myself. Then send it to the home office in Los Angeles."

They viewed the video and agreed it was fantastic in every way. Ted sent it to the home office and the two celebrated their achievement.

"I'd love to see the look on old man Skinners face when he sees a 65-foot Komodo Dragon eating people and demolishing buildings," John said.

It was indeed worth a million dollars to watch as head editor Lew Skinner viewed the historical footage. He was speechless as he watched, which was unbelievable if you knew the man.

"Send Sam Tallow a message. Tell him to shoot more, more, more," editor Skinner ordered intern Mary Rush.

"Yes sir, right away," she replied.

The footage was shown that night on the 6 o'clock news and within 15 minutes it was picked up by all the major networks. It spread throughout social media faster than any bullet being fired at the target range.

The situation of a mutated lizard was out of the box and spreading throughout the world's public citizenries. The overall public still had no clue of the mutated shark and whale attacks.

INSTITUTE FOR OCEANOGRAPHY

Dr. Tylor watched intensely as the Komodo Dragon footage was being shown on the islands evening cable news. He was worried and concerned that there would be other undetected developments to follow. He was at a lost to narrow any hypothesis down to the one most promising.

Dr. Tylor called Eric Sloan and inquired how the investigation into the shark attacks was progressing. He was thrilled by the news that Captain Bomber had killed a Great White and that a large piece of the carcass was being studied at the CDC.

As soon as Dr. Tylor's call ended, the phone rang.

"Hello," he said.

"Dr. Tylor, Bill Wilson here. I suppose you've heard about the Komodo Dragon incident? I read the report that Captain Toma wired me. I agreed with his assessment that there's not much you can do at this point.

I'm meeting with experts to discuss how to obtain some samples from one of the mutated whales for scientific analysis. You know those damn Green Peace environmentalist will be screaming their lungs out if we even lay a finger on one.

That's my problem, not yours. I've got a helicopter coming from Elmendorf Air Force Base to pick you up. It should be there within the hour. I've got a jet on standby to fly you down to the Galapagos Islands.

Meet up with a reporter named Sam Tallow. I've called his boss and advised him to allow Mr. Tallow to cooperate with you fully. See what you can find out how this could have happened and how long it's been going on.

In the meantime, I will be out of the country. I've got important State Department business abroad. I just sent you my private cell number in case an emergency arises. I'll be back in three days. If I'll be longer, I'll give you a call. Be carful Dr. I'll talk to you later."

Dr. Tylor hung up the phone and notified the hotel clerk he was checking out. It took only a few minutes to pack his belongings. There was a knock at the door and as he opened it, he saw Captain Toma.

"Ready to go Dr? I'll drive you down to the helipad. The pilot notified me he was 15 minutes out. He wants to land and burn. There's bad weather coming in fast."

"Yes, I'm ready Captain. It was a pleasure to meet you and the men and women in your department. It's beautiful here. I would like to come back on my vacation and spend a couple of weeks enjoying the serenity. That's after this whale situation is over."

Both men had a smirk, realizing that serenity didn't exist currently.

The chopper landed and the wind it created was stingingly cold. Dr. Tylor hurried inside and gave Captain Toma a wave as the helicopter rose and banked towards the north.

The chopper landed about 150 feet away from the F-15 that was ready for departure.

Dr. Tylor enjoyed the view as the jet sped over the Pacific at Mach 1. He enjoyed witnessing the three-midair refueling maneuverers. The distance from Alaska to the Galapagos Islands is 7,400 miles. The F-15 has a range of 1900 miles, so the midair refueling were done to complete their mission as fast as possible.

The State Department had cleared access to fly in different countries restricted airspace. It wasn't easy for Latin American countries to allow an American F-15 to fly over their airspace. If it hadn't been for the Komodo Dragon situation, it would have been near impossible to gain their permission.

Once landing in Quito, Ecuador Dr. Tylor took an air shuttle hopper to Manta, Ecuador and then a helicopter ride to the city of Puerto Villamill, one of a few in the Galapagos Island chain.

There was only one small hotel, (that's what it was called by this remote standards). Dr. Tylor walked into the lobby and was immediately met by reporter Sam Tallow.

"You must be Dr. Tylor from the Institute of Oceanography?" I'm Sam Tallow. And that dude over there at the bar is my cameraman Ted Wilcox. We were ordered to be at your beckon call.

It's not that I don't want to babysit you, but it hinders my investigating and reporting my story."

"You've got it backwards Mr. Tallow. I'm going to follow you around and document your findings. I will ask you a question from time to time, if that's okay with you. I'm not here to feed my ego or make a name for myself.

I'm here to find out what has caused these creatures to triple or quadruple in size. I seek the same answers that you probably do. Where are they nesting? What are they eating, on such a small island? Are they going to continue to grow in size and if they are, how much larger? Aren't these the questions you want answers to?"

"Yes, they are. If that's the way this symbiotic relationship will be conducted, we will get along fine. Be ready at 5 AM, I have a jeep and we're going dragon hunting."

THE DECEPTIVE

Captain Bomber and his crew were carrying out a black op mission. Only a small handful of highly placed individuals had the security clearance to have knowledge of its orders.

The Deceptive was carrying a special harpoon spear. It was modified to be shot out one of its torpedo tubes. Once it was fired and struck its target, a homing device would be injected into the shark.

Even though a ships torpedo tubes are much smaller than on a submarine. This modified weapon was designed for the 13-inch tubes on the Deceptive.

The government wanted to track the movement of the mutated creatures. Researchers needed to know how deep they could go. They were also concerned with the distance that they were occupying in the Pacific.

The fact that only the government was aware of the three separate incidents, did make their job easier than being harassed by public demonstrators.

After four days of searching for one of the mutated sharks. One found them. The shark came straight up from the deep and rammed the Deceptive in its midsection from below.

The ship was literally lifted up eight to ten feet into the air. It splashed back down with such tremendous force that it threw everyone to the deck.

"Man, your stations." yelled Captain Bomber as he struggled to his feet.

"Sonar, where the hell is that bastard?"

"I've got him Captain. He's 1000 yards off the portside."

"Helmsman, bring us around portside and line us up to fire the spear. I want this son-of-a-bitch. Sonar, you keep that target dead in front of our firing sight and range. Is that clear sailor?"

"Yes, Captain. He's out running us Captain. We need more speed to keep him in firing range."

"Engine room, this is your Captain. Full speed ahead until I give you orders to disengage."

"Yes, Captain, full speed ahead sir."

"Captain we're in range and target the is locked on," said sonar tech Brad Miller.

"Ready to fire on my command." Captain Bomber said.

"900, 800, 700 yards," said Seaman Miller

"FIRE." Captain Bomber ordered.

The weaponized spear was launched from the on-deck torpedo tube. It took a couple of seconds for the spear's impact with the shark to occur. When it struck the massive shark the tracking beacon was implanted. The shark had absolutely no reaction to it being injected.

"Communications, is the tracking device functional?" Asked the Captain

"Engine room, half speed" Captain Bomber ordered.

"Yes Captain, the tracking signal is strong and active. I was told by the N S A that this signal will work at any depth or distance. There is nowhere that we can't track the signals location," said Communication Tech Jimmy Barns.

"Good job gentlemen. We deserve our shore leave. Helmsmen, make our course for home base, Hawaii." Captain Bomber said as the crew cheered.

PUERTO VILLAMIL

Next morning Sam Tallow and Dr. John Tylor jumped into their rented four door Rubicon jeep, filled with anticipation. Sam drove to a location that he knew was a mating site for the Komodo's.

Sam had brought along two high powered rifles for their protection if needed. Dr. Tylor wasn't fond of weapons of any kind. However, he did see a cause for alarm and the possibility that their presents could be lifesaving.

It took a short time to reach an isolated area of the island where Sam thought the Komodo's might be. As they stepped out of the vehicle, they heard a rustling in the heavy brush. They got back into the jeep and started the engine.

"Better safe than sorry Doctor," Sam said

It was a good thing they retreated. A hundred yards away, an 80-foot Komodo Dragon slowly walked out of the brush. He didn't charge them. He just stood there flicking his tongue repeatedly, covering a twenty-foot distance.

It was a stand off until a wild pig ran across their path. Like lightening the Komodo jumped forward and with its huge long tongue grabbed the pig. In an instant the pig disappeared in one gulp as the dragon swallowed it whole.

Being that the reptile had eaten, he turned and disappeared back into the underbrush. Sam and Dr. Tylor waited for half an hour before once again exiting the vehicle. This time both had a weapon slung across their shoulder.

They quietly advanced through the brush with their heads on a swivel watching each other's six. Dr. Tylor had sweat rolling down his brow, burning his eyes as the driblets made contact.

It didn't take long (fortunately) before Sam found what he was looking for. He dropped to his knees and starting digging with his hands rapidly. He uncovered several eggs that had been hidden by a female.

"How many do you need Dr. for your studies?"

"Six should be enough Sam. I want to send one to the CDC and Dr. Zurich. He's the paleontologist that works with the government on secretive projects. Dr. Zurich works with the cellular structure of Dinosaurs and fossils. He might see some resemblance with his knowledge."

"Six it is Doc."

John gently placed six eggs into a cloth bag and then covered the remaining eggs back over. They were finally able to take a sigh of relief, once they were safely driving back to the city.

Once back to the Hilton Hotel, Dr. Tylor packaged the eggs in bubble wrap and cloth.

While he was doing that, Sam called Bill Wilson and informed him of their find and what Dr. Tylor had suggested.

Bill immediately made arrangements for the egg's deliveries to the addresses that Dr. Tylor had listed.

As soon as the eggs were ready to ship, Dr. Tylor and Sam met the Navy's Sea Ranger helicopter that had landed in the hotels parking lot. The eggs and Dr. Tylor boarded the chopper and it flew off back to Quito, Ecuador.

The minute that it touched down at the Quito airfield. The different packages were distributed among three different F-15's. One blasted off for the CDC in Atlanta, Ga. Another one for Dr. Zurich at the secret location of his lab. (only high security clearance personnel allowed). The last one blasted off to another secret location. This one was for the State Department eyes only.

Dr, Tylor had kept one egg for his research. He asked for and was granted permission to return to his office at the Institute of

Oceanography. As he watched the three F-15's depart he noticed another, but different type of jet landing. It taxied up to him and the canopy opened.

The pilot lowered a ladder and motioned for Dr. Tylor to get onboard. He climbed into the back seat and buckled in for the ride back to Hawaii.

THE CELL

As Dr. Tylor was in transit to Alaska, he pondered where the undisclosed location might be that the third jet was headed. He thought about several prominent men and women that were qualified to analyze and be trusted with such a matter.

At about the same time Dr. Tylor touched down at Elmendorf Air Force Base. the jet that he had been thinking about was also wheels down in a secret location.

The United States State Department has many publicly unknown locations. This particular facility was nicknamed, THE CELL. It was one that focused on tissue analyzes, genetics, cellular mutations, viruses and anything that was deemed to be of unknown nature.

Dr. Erica Jones is not only head of THE CELL, she is also the worlds most renowned authority in this field of research. She represents the true definition of being a doyen.

She met the F-15 on the tarmac herself and took procession of the two eggs that had been sent to her. With her assigned heavy security by her side, she retreated to the level 4 laboratories that were 120 feet below the surface.

She had a crew of 14 scientist already assembled and waiting to start their investigation into the egg's cellular makeup. Dr. Jones handed one egg to Dr. Clay Wang, for him and the others to disperse among themselves. That way they could run 14 different tests at the same time.

She kept the other egg for herself. She weighed it, X-rayed it and measured it. She made the decision not to crack it open to gain access to the yoke and materials inside the shell. She inserted two needles and drew out some yoke in one and the white in the other.

She immediately put the samples on a slide. She wanted to view the yoke cells first. She put the slide under the electron microscope for viewing. As she looked through the eyesight's and focused the image to its highest magnification of 10,000,000x, she was astounded.

What she saw was unexplainable and left her speechless for a minute. It wasn't because the cells were mutated. It was that there were three completely separate types of mutated cells. Each variety differently mutated than the other types. Each independent from the others.

She was almost afraid to check the next sample of the white fluid from inside the shell. She removed the yoke slide from under the microscope. She cautiously placed the next sample under the microscope and began focusing the image.

"NO! THIS ISN'T POSSIABLE." Dr. Jones uttered loudly.

Dr. Wang came running to see what Dr. Jones was shouting about.

"What's wrong, Dr?" He asked her.

"Look at this, and tell me what you see Dr. Wang?"

He viewed the images and immediately stood up and tilted his head in amazement.

"I see three separate types of cells that are independent from the others and mutated in their own identity."

"Now look at this slide and tell me what you see?"

Dr. Wang removed the slide and replaced it with the slide with yoke cells on it. He focused the image to his viewing sharpness.

"WHAT THE HELL?" Dr. Wang yelled.

"Tell me, what did you see?"

"The same as the other slide. The three different cells, muted in their own identities."

"Anything else, Dr Wang?"

"No, is there something I'm missing Dr. Jones?"

"Look at the other slide again and really stare at it. Then tell me what you see? What does it have in common with the other slide?"

Dr. Wang looked at the pervious slide once again. He stared at it in silence. He was feeling the pressure of not seeing whatever it was that

Dr. Jones had discovered. He stood erect and wiped his eyes and bent back over the microscope.

"OH DAMN. I see it now. This has life threating indications. I mean for all of life as we know it."

"I agree, Dr. Wang, but I need to hear you explain to me what you saw."

"The three different cell types on this slide is totally different than the three different cell types on the other slide. That gives us six totally different mutated cell types with six totally different mutations. Nothing matches with any other entity, yet they are cohabitating and developing a new species."

"Correct and that scares me to death. This could be the start of earths Armageddon. I know this sounds crazy; but what if this is an alien genetic experiment? There has to be a logical explanation scientifically and not some concocted theory of being of extraterrestrial origin.

Everyone, gather here. I want these cells, tissue samples and DNA put through every test we know. Heat, freeze, burn, bombard them with lasers, light, dry ice. Hell, do what ever you want, pour chocolate on the damn things for all I care. Bottom line people. Find out what the hell we're dealing with ASAP. Life as we know it, really is in immediate danger."

The 14 experts, each in their own scientific fields, dispersed with Dr. Jones's haunting tone of Armageddon ringing in their ears.

Dr. Jones herself started her own avenue of inquiry. She lined up several samples, each one in a petri dish. With an eyedropper she put one drop of iodine on the first sample and studied the results under the electron microscope.

She made note of the findings and moved to the second sample. She put one drop of a combination wood and grain alcohol.

She looked up and saw her research team conducting a variety of test. Dr. Wang was doing microwave experiments, while a trio of scientist were conducting X-ray saturation tests and monitoring their reactions.

The ability to solve or even understand the task at hand, consisted of literally 1000's of complex equations and dealt with several of the sciences. A botanist, biologist, an expert in herbalism and without a doubt, a mathematician. A person that's an expert in Dynamical Systems & Differential Equations and Physics.

The challenge that faces the team members at THE CELL in laymen terms basically.

DNA molecules are very long. They can't fit in a cell without becoming coiled tightly. Once the DNA molecule completes it's coiling, it becomes a structure. That structure is called a chromosome.

Humans have 23 pairs of chromosomes inside a cell's nucleus. It takes approximately 1000 genes to make one strand of DNA. The chemical structure in DNA is a Double Helix, which means there are 46 chromosomes.

I'm know nothing about how all this works. I know you can see the complexity of DNA, genes and what it takes for humans to exist. All that and much more beyond my capability or understanding is a person's makeup.

Now you can see how six different cellular configurations and DNA's could easily take years and years, if even possible to solve.

Enough of hearing about stuff that most of us don't understand. I think that's all I need to say about what is taking place at THE CELL.

INSTITUTE FOR OCEANOGHAPHY

Dr. Tylor felt queasy as the wheels touched down on the runway at the Joint Base Pearl Harbor-Hickam in Hawaii. It was the first time that a civilian was permitted to fly in a F35B Lightning II fighter jet. He felt privileged and honored for having that accomplishment, but he was too sick at the time to celebrate the fact.

He had suffered too many hours working and being hurriedly flown off to different locations with no days off in-between. Dr. Tylor isn't what one might say is old, but he was in his late sixties and became fatigued easily.

He went straight to his office and laid down in the bed that was in his private resting room. It was closer and faster than going all the way home. He dozed off the minute his head made contact with the pillow. He had for the first time in many days a smile of contentment on his face.

SYDNEY AUSTRALIA

Josh Hopper hurried up to the docks in Sydney and moored his boat while yelling out to call 911. Several people on the dock started calling 911 as Josh had ordered.

"HELP! Will someone help me carry my friend up to the landing area so the ambulance can save time?" Josh said.

A couple of men helped Josh carry his friend Kevin Trotter up the ramp and next to the parking lot.

As they laid him down gently, they heard the sirens of the ambulance approaching. Within a few seconds it came to an abrupt stop in front of Josh and the crowd of people that had gathered.

"He got stung by a Portuguese Man of War. It was the biggest jellyfish I've ever seen." Josh explained to the EMT's.

The two men applied the proper treatment for such stings; but weren't having much in the way of favorable results. They stabilized their patient the best they could and sped off for the hospital.

Josh followed behind the ambulance all the way to the hospital. He saw them rush Kevin down the hallway and into a room. Several medical personnel hurriedly entered the room.

Josh waited to find out the condition of his friend. He answered questions about his friend's name, address, etc.

He hadn't waited very long until he was approached by a doctor.

"Hello, I'm Dr. Howard Shaw and I understand you're a close friend of Kevin Trotter and that he has no family to call or notify."

"Yes, that's correct. Kevin's family were killed in an automobile accident four years ago. He's single and has no brothers, sisters, aunts, uncles or any distant relatives that he is aware of."

"I'm sorry to say that he died on the examining table a few minutes ago. We did everything we could; but he had so much venom in his system, there wasn't anything we could do.

I saw the sting marks all over his body. How did he acquire so many? They were huge in comparison to what I usually see in a jellyfish attack."

"Dr. Shaw, I don't know how much you know about jellyfish. A normal looking Portuguese-Man-of War is 12 inches long, 5 inches wide and has tentacles as long as 150 feet.

The one that attacked Kevin was at least 36 inches long, 16 inches wide and God only knows how long its tentacles were.

Our ice chest fell overboard and Kevin dove into the water to retrieve it. I saw this huge bubble of water start coming straight for him. I started screaming for him to get back in the boat. I kept yelling, hurry, hurry, but he couldn't out swim what was tracking him.

Kevin had just reached the side of the boat when he started screaming. I tried to pull him inside the boat. He had gone limp and was unconscious. It took all my might to pull him into the boat.

I saw what had attacked him. Kevin didn't swim into the jellyfish. I swear to you, that damn thing attacked him.

Josh hadn't been paying any attention to the people gathered behind him. It was the Sydney press core. They were filming video and clicking pictures. When they heard the jellyfish's size that Josh described, that was a major story.

Within two hours the story had been picked up by all the major news outlets. By the next day stories of other unexplainable attacks somehow were leaked to the press.

In less than 24 hours the world was aware of incidents in Sydney Australia, Kodiac Island, Alaska, Puerto Villamil, Galapagos and in the South Pacific around the Mariana Trench.

Fear around the world rose to a staggering level. People were afraid to play, fish or put a boat in the water.

Over the next week, reports of strange occurrences were being reported from Japan, Honduras, Greenland and other locations.

It had been suggested that the radiation from the Japanese, Fukushima Nuclear Power Plant disaster on March 11 in 2011 was a strong possibility for the cause of these mutations.

It was true that higher radiation levels in the Pacific had been reported by Hawaii, California, Oregon and Washington State. However, that would be a farfetched theory to explain the incidents in Greenland, Honduras and all Atlantic Ocean occurrences.

However, it did warrant a new research group to be formed. Its purpose was to study tides, ocean currents, water temperatures and even the jet stream in case a mutated form of pollination was taking place.

President Black appointed Dr. Thomas Elvan, formerly head of the United States Weather Bureau; to the position head of Species Migration Patterns. He was highly recommended by Dr. Tylor and that played a major part in the Presidents final decision.

Dr. Elvan set up an office in the outskirts of D C and selected his team. President Black had given him the authority to assemble who he thought were best for the team. The President also gave him the power to purchase. There was only one stipulation. The research groups financial budget approval was only 100 million dollars.

THE SECRET
WORLD BELOW

The Lithosphere area of earth's core is the coolest part of earth's mantle. It's reaches its deepest depth of miles before the next transition that's hotter. In the upper section of the Lithosphere, (existence unknown to the surface world) are several cities that are inhabited by an extraordinary race.

They survive somewhere in a comfort zone, suitable for their survival.

The Lithosphere comes closest to the surface around 24.85 miles (40 km) deep. The temperature can be low as -89 C (-128.20 degrees Fahrenheit) At its deepest point of 173.98 miles (280 km) the temperature can reach 1,112 degrees Fahrenheit.

Somewhere in that 149.13 mile depth is home to a race called Gorack.

The most beneficial aspect of the Lithosphere layer is that there is more water contained within its boundaries than all the water on the surface.

The Gorack have lived for thousands of years underground undetected. The fact is that they monitor the earth's functions. Many they can alter or control. There are others they too have to endure along with the rest of us.

Eighty percent of the volcanic eruptions on the surface are deliberately set in motion by the Gorack. The ocean floor is covered with volcanic vents that are constantly spewing gases and magma.

They serve as pressure valves that release deeper internal pressure, hundreds of miles deeper. If the pressure was allowed to build up with no safety valve. Earth would explode like a balloon stuck with a pin.

Whenever the sea vents can't release pressure fast enough, The Gorack trigger a volcanic eruption nearest to wherever the pressure bulge is growing.

The Gorack have been filtering water forever it seems. That's why we enjoy clean well water and especially Artesian Wells.

The metabolism of the Gorack has changed repeatedly over centuries to help them in the adaptation process in order to conquer their environment.

The Gorack used steam vents to cook their meals. Where their food comes from or what it is, is still a mystery.

"Come and help me with deciphering these readings, Follower Jong," said Rodic, the Supreme Leader.

One thing of great importance, is that the Gorack do not have sub-servant tendencies. No one address's another by their title or rank. That doesn't mean they don't respect the office or position.

They know the status of the one they are addressing and it's their tone and body language that says it all.

"I'm coming Rodic. How can I help?"

"Open valve number 6 when I close down valve 14. We have to synchronize our movements. Turn on three. One, two THREE."

They both implemented their assigned duty to a successful conclusion.

"Thank you, Jong. Pressure was building up under Mount Rainer, Mount Lassen and Crater Lake.

People in the Pacific Northwest don't know how valuable Crater Lake is to their safety. If the lake wasn't there and only the deep crater, they would be inundated with several earthquakes every decade.

Except for the Mount Saint Helens eruption, there hasn't been a major 7 or above quake. Look at the huge quakes in southern California and Alaska. Except for Mount Saint Helens, the other mountains in the chain have only small tremors.

Mount Rainer, Mount Adams, Mount Hood, Mount Bachelor, Sisters, Mount Shasta, Crater Lake and Mount Lassen.

The reason is the cold water in Crater Lake helps to control the earths temperature. The Pacific Ocean cools the westside of the Rockies. Crater Lake cools the eastside of the Rockies and helps cooling from Mount Rainer to Mount Lassen.

The Pacific Northwest is the easiest place on earth to manage. I'll leave you in charge of this level one, Area 47, follower Jong. I'm going to level three and monitor the El Misti volcano in Peru, from area 87.

The Gorack live on three levels that over the years they have created. Levels one and two are the areas that watch the North and South Americas along with all the Asian probabilities.

Level two monitors the rest of the world. But it focused on Tibet and China somewhat more than other areas, due to the number of earthquakes in that region.

The Gorack's are humanoid, but with some modifications or mutation if you prefer. Their skin is white as white can become. Their hair is long and white as could be as well.

They have huge eyes and are mostly blue. However, there are a few that have pink or red eyes. They reproduce exactly as any other Homosapien couple would.

The Gorack society have adapted to their underworld life by using geothermal to their advantage. Not only are there volcanic vents, there are thousands of geothermal (or steam) vents.

Over the thousands of years, the Gorack have existed, they have harnessed geothermal to its maximum use. They not only cook with it, but it makes enough energy for them to have low voltage electricity.

That electrical output is just enough to manage the monitoring stations with a very low amount of light. The lights are methane gas and glow when tiny amount of voltage is being introduced.

The source of the Gorack's energy is many paddlewheels placed over hundreds of geothermal vents, that spin the blades.

The monitoring stations are rudimental, but effective. Ever station has several one-inch tubes, each one represents a specific zone. The Gorack's have found that by putting a certain amount of mud into the tubes as a plug, that when the pressure builds to a certain amount, the mud plug would be pushed out, alerting them to the possible upcoming event.

When that happens, the decision is made what valves to be turned and how many to divert pressure away from the alerted area.

At this time, no one on the surface knew or even suspected there were people living far within the earths surface.

What's the question that represents the elephant in the room? Answer, what do the Gorack's have to do with the mutated creatures above?

HAWAII

Dr. Tylor was awaking by a loud pounding on the front door of the Institute of Oceanography. He rose and approached the door. He opened it and a UPS person was standing there.

"Are you Dr. Tylor?"

"Yes."

"Sign here please, I have an official envelope for you sir."

Dr. Tylor signed, nodded, took the delivery and closed the door. He opened the manila envelope and was surprise to see the test results had come back so fast.

The results along with a summery were from Dr. Zurich at the CDC.

He thumbed through the pages while making a fresh cup of coffee. His mental ability understood the situation, but he thought it impossible. No way could something like this ever be reality. This was a situation you'd only find in a science fiction novel.

He thought there had to be a mistake. He couldn't believe Dr. Zurich could make such a mistake. He called the CDC and spoke to Dr. Zurich.

"Dr. Zurich, Dr. Tylor here. I just received your findings on the samples you tested. You tested samples from Alaska, Puerto Villamil, the Deceptive and Australia?"

"That's correct Dr. Tylor. I know what you're thinking. I can assure you that everyone in this lab have doubled checked their findings. Then we doubled checked each other's results. You are welcome to come to my lab and we can go over the results together."

"Thank you so much Dr. Zurich. I would love to work alongside someone of your undisputed reputation. Please, don't think I'm doubting your qualifications. This is so unbelievable; I've got to see these six independent strands of DNA. Three individual strands located on each side of the Double Helix. I have to physically see it with my own eyes Dr. It's such a monumental discovery."

"I agree Dr Tylor. Come on out to Georgia and join me in my lab. I'll try and answer any question you might have."

"Thank you, Dr. Zurich. I'll leave as soon as I can book a flight. I don't think the government will fly me free so I can satisfy something that's of my personal nature."

ATLANTA

Landing in Atlanta, Georgia wasn't smooth at all. It usually includes some turbulence and lightning flashes. Dr. Tylor gripped the arms of his seat as the plane started its descent.

He got bounced around and shook side to side, but a feeling of relief spread across his face once he was safely back on the ground.

He was amused for some reason riding the no operater train car to the main terminal. He went to the baggage claim area and started looking for his baggage.

As he pulled his suitcase from the revolving carousel, he heard his name being called out over the intercom system.

"Dr. John Tylor, please report to the security desk located in the main lobby area."

Dr. Tylor had to ask one of the security officers that monitor the airport where exactly the security booth was.

The Atlanta Hartsfield-Jackson International Airport is huge and you can get easily turned around and lost.

The security officer hailed one of the many transport vehicles for Dr. Tylor to ride. He was grateful for that gestor. It turned out that his destination was all the way across the terminal.

Upon arrival at said location he noticed a man holding a sign with his name printed on it.

"Hello, I'm Dr. Tylor."

"Pleasure to meet you sir. I am your driver and I'll drive you to the CDC facility," He said.

Once outside the terminal a skycap opened the door to a white stretch limousine.

"Is this for me?" Dr. Tylor asked.

The sky cap nodded affirmably and Dr. Tylor handed him a twenty-dollar bill.

The limo sped away from the curb and merged with the outgoing traffic.

"I didn't catch your name,"

"Oh, my apologies sir. I'm Brent Smith and I work as a drive with Classic Limousine Service. I have had this job for 16 years as of this week. I am assigned to drive for movie stars, rock stars, politicians and VIP's."

"How did I happen to get you as my driver? I sure don't fit your normal clientele Brent."

"Quite the contrary Dr. You are one of the highly noted doctors along with several brilliant scientist that are gathering at the CDC.

I'm told that the greatest minds of the world were summoned to a meeting of great importance at the CDC. You see Dr. Tylor, you are more important than a movie star, rock star, professional athlete or politician.

I don't know the crisis that's facing us, but it must be massive if the biggest guns on earth are coming together."

"I'm here for a friendly visit with Dr. Zurich. I not aware of anything to be concerned about. You know how rumors are? You can't believe even half of what they say."

"You may be right Doc, but one has to be concerned. This is not a seminar or convention. These highly qualified people certainly are not on sabbaticals at one time.

I know you couldn't say something even if there were a crisis. We're here Dr. Tylor. Take my card. I'm your designated driver 24-7, night or day. As long as you are in Atlanta, I am only to drive you."

"Thank you, Brent," said Dr. Tylor as he put the card in his shirt pocket.

The Dr. walked through the revolving door of the lobby and was met by a beautiful woman.

"Dr. Tylor, I'm Sarah Winters, Dr. Zurich's personnel assistance. We have fine accommodations here on site if you prefer. A 5-star hotel is several minutes away and with traffic you could be delayed for who knows how long. The choice is yours."

"Thank you, miss. I don't need a 5-star hotel."

"Dr. Tylor, all guest of the CDC are always booked in a 5-star accommodation. Dr. Zurich considers you a guest and colleague. He feels you are a valuable asset or he wouldn't have invited you to his lab.

Trust me Dr. Tylor. Very few people other than his research team have been allowed into his private lab. There are many doctors working here. I bet only two or three at the most have been inside his lab. You are the first outsider to be allowed to witness what you're going to see."

"Wow, that's a lot for me to absorb. But as I stated, your accommodations here in the CDC facility will be just fine."

"Ok then. Follow me and I'll show you the decontamination chamber."

After a short walk they entered what was labeled a private elevator. Dr. Tylor noticed that it took a black embossed card with a triangle hologram on it for Sarah to obtain entry.

"This is the only access to Dr. Zurich's level 4 lab. There are six exits from the lab in case of a breach or safety issue arises. You can get out through them, but you can't use them as an entry point." Sarah said.

The elevator went down and down for what seemed like forever for Dr. Tylor. It finally came to a stop and the door slid open. They stepped out of the elevator and a man was standing there in a protective suit.

"This is Dr. Jimmy Stoner and he will take over from here. As long as you are here at level 4, he is your contact. Never go anywhere alone. A CDC person must accompany you at all times, NO! Exceptions!" Sarah said as the elevator door slide shut.

"Follow me Doc. You can undress in there. Take a disinfectant shower over there. I'll lay your clothes here and I'll wait outside the door." Jimmy said.

In a half an hour, Dr. Tylor exited the staging room dressed in the protective suit.

"Man, it's hotter than hell in this thing," he said.

"You'll get used to it after a while. Once inside the lab, you'll be hooked up to air and you'll be cool in minutes."

"Great."

Jimmy lead the way to the double door entry to the lab. "Dr. Tylor, go through this door and wait for 15 seconds. Then the next door opens and allows you to enter into the lab."

Dr. Tylor did as he was instructed. He entered through the first door and as it closed, he was bombard with a forceful spray from all angles. When the spay stopped, the next door opened and he stepped into Dr. Zurich's level 4 lab.

"Great to finally meet you Dr. Tylor, welcome to my domain." Dr Zurich said.

"Thank you so much for granting me this honor Dr. Zurich."

"Let's get something straight right now. We don't bother with titles and who's better than another down here. Everyone calls me Doc and if it's ok with you, I'll refer to you as John."

"You've got it, Doc."

"I've got samples laid out over here. I thought we would start from the beginning so you can see from the start how we arrived at our results."

The two of them began placing samples on slides and putting other samples in petri dishes.

THE CELL

Dr. Erica Jones notified Bill Wilson of the State Department that she would like to make contact with Dr. Zurich at the CDC.

"Listen Bill, I want to compare notes with Doc. We've been friends for so many years, I can't count that far."

"Who?" Bill questioned.

"Dr. Zurich at the CDC. Get with the program Bill. I sent you an e-mail about my request or didn't you even check you e-mail?"

"I got your e-mail and it didn't say anything about a Doc. How in hell am I suppose to know that's Dr. Zurich."

"Why do you need my approval to contact him? You said your friends, just call him up and talk."

"Oh, you would just love that. I need your permission so I can talk on a secured private line. Would you rather me give him a call on my Verizon cell phone and discus our little problem?"

"Hell no. I see your point. You have permission and the authority to use the green phone to call the CDC's green phone."

"Thank you, Bill. Now that wasn't so hard was it?"

I'll let Homeland Security know your calling. How about 20 minutes from now to place your call?"

"That will work, Bill. Thanks."

PUERTO VILLAMIL

Sam Tallow was reaching out to the Ecuadorian Government for special permission to shoot and kill Komodo Dragons in the Galapagos Island Chain.

The dragons are on the venerable or threatened list, but not on the endangered list.

He also was in contact with NOAA. He was asking the U S to help convince the Ecuadorian Government to allow this extreme action.

The Komodo's were eating everything on the islands. There were more and more Komodo's every week and they were still growing.

The fear was that once the food supply was exhausted, the dragons would be forced to swim to Peru, Chile, Ecuador and other South American countries.

Sam was the only person still left on the island. He was in a lookout stations 75 feet above the surface. If he were to be discovered by a dragon, it could easily kill him in a couple of seconds after being detected.

He was now trapped. There were dozens of Komodo Dragons roaming the entire island. He could never reach the water and take a boat to safety. Besides, the dragons are excellent swimmers.

The two governments were still debating over how to reach a decision both could agree on.

Sam had made arrangements for a helicopter to rescue him. As the sun was starting to sink beneath the horizon the chopper arrived. As it lowered a basket for him to get in, a mammoth Komodo saw Sam in the station.

With its tongue flickering, it charged the wooden structure. As its tongue touched the bottom of Sam's boot, he was jerked upward by the helicopter leaving.

The higher the chopper rose, the more Sam could see how over populated the island was with Komodo's. He knew there was no place for them to go but the main land. He filmed what he could with his iPhone. He thought it would make the two governments quickly arrive at a solution.

ALASKA, KODIAC ISLAND

Captain Tome was being challenged by high winds and waves in the Bearing Sea. He and his crew were assigned to attach tracker devices on at least 10 more Orcas.

Under normal conditions, Captain Tome wouldn't put his boat or crew in such a dangerous situation. He had no input in the decision to risk everything and go find whales and attach the devices.

The Coast Guard works with the Navy when asked. It also answers to the Department of Homeland Security. It was Homelands orders to leave port and pursue the Orcas.

Trust me, you don't question the Department of Homeland Security. When they say jump, you really do say how high and then ask when you can come down.

You've heard the saying, (too many cooks in the kitchen spoils the broth). One could say that about this situation. But because of the severity of being an Armageddon moment, it was all hands-on deck.

Once Captain Tome's boat cleared the harbor and the 15-foot breakwater waves. He was notified on his satellite phone that Homeland Security had issued to everyone that worked on the issue, that Homeland Security officials had told them to start referring to the issue as Project Discover and that Dr. John Tylor had been assigned its Director.

Due to heavy seas, it took three hours instead of two, to reach Stutters Fault. It didn't take long before they were being rapidly pushed forward. Captain Tome rushed to the back of the boat and fired the specially built rifle that projected the tracking device.

The kickback nearly knocked him to the deck. He hadn't anticipated it being that powerful. His shot was a direct hit and he could see by the amount of the firing bolt that stuck out, it was deep and affixed solidly.

"One down and nine to go. Make sure we have a strong signal, Seaman Chris." Captain Tome said.

"Yes, Captain. The signal is strong and functioning perfectly," he answered.

The boat suddenly returned to its normal speed. The Orca had quit pushing and sonar showed it diving deep down into the depths of Stutters Fault.

"I don't understand why these mammals bump and run. It's pushing us and not destroying us. It's like they want to play and have fun like a puppy.

The destruction of the boats earlier was because they were small and couldn't withstand being battered around. The only reports now are attacks on submarines, large tankers. There's only one cruise ship still operating and it hasn't reported any contact.

Our Coast Guard boat must be the perfect size to literally play with safely. You saw the enormous size of the creature. It could easily swallow this boat with ease. One swipe of its tail and we would be a pile of toothpicks. There's more going on here than meets the eye. Let's continue with our orders at hand. I want to watch how we are treated by each of these creatures."

PUERTO VILLAMIL, GALAPAGOS

The Komodo Dragons were turning on each other, due to the fact that all food had been devoured. Homeland Security had ordered that the Galapagos Island chain be under a 24 x 7 watch.

As a Coast Guard helicopter flew over Puerto Villamil, the spotter noticed an alarming scene. A large bank of Komodo Dragons was slithering into the ocean. There had to be at least 100 of the big lizards in the water. They were swimming towards Ecuador. That distance is only 62 miles and Komodo's are excellent swimmers.

The helicopter pilot immediately took video of the movement and forward it and his report to Homeland Security. It was obvious that time for stalling or trying to gain political favoritism, had ran out.

Something had to be decided fast. The United States had already settled on an action to neutralize the dragons and protect the people, if the Ecuadorian government refused to negotiate honestly.

Green Peace, PETA and other animal rights groups were picketing and protesting any action that might hurt the animals. Whereas the Ecuador government was worried about protecting its tourist image and revenue.

The Komodo's were already half way to an Ecuadorian beach. These Lizards were an unbelievable 185 feet long and 16 feet tall when pushed up on their front legs.

Time was running out and since the Ecuadorian government kept bickering back and forth with the United States negotiating team, the U S set their plan quietly in motion.

THE CELL

"Dr Jones, this is the most fantastic lab setup I've ever seen. You have every piece of research equipment that exists. You've even got some tools that aren't even available because they are prototypes." John stated.

"Yes, it's good to be a renown Doctor in my field and work at The Cell. I want you to analyze this double helix and tell me what you conclude it to be."

"I really don't see any difference between the two."

"You're right John, I didn't either. It was Dr. Mote, he's the head of genetics and gene research. He specializes in prehistoric genealogy and its DNA.

Dr. Mote, would you be so kind as to join Dr. Tylor and me?"

"It's a pleasure to meet you Dr. Tylor. I'm Dr. Rip Mote."

"Pleasure to meet you as well Dr." John responded.

"Rip, would you explain your findings after your initial evaluation?" Erica asked.

"I'd love to Dr. When you first look at the two cell samples side by side under the electron microscope, you can't decipher between them. Theoretically, what I did should have not rendered any kind of results.

Dr. Jones told us to think outside the box and try any and all thoughts, no matter how off the wall they were. I removed the white light from the electron microscope and replaced it with a black light.

I've still got that procedure active on my electron microscope. Follow me and you can see for yourself.

Go ahead Dr. Tylor and have a look. As you can now see the edges of one of the cells are smooth. While the other one has minute notches around its edges, just like a quarter or dime.

I have seen this exact trait many times during my years of researching dinosaurs and their DNA. These cells may be from today's creatures; but they somehow have prehistoric DNA in them. I am studying the genetic trail from dinosaurs to caveman to present, for a clue why this is happening now.

If the next generation of these mutated species have more of this prehistoric DNA. The world may very well be in it's last days as we know it."

THE SECRET
WORLD BELOW

Rodic sat in the transfer vehicle that was used to travel between monitoring stations. It was the work of geniuses in many ways.

The floor of the volcanic tubes had a slot in them. A hook coupler projected out of the slot. The hook attached to the front of the transport vehicle. When the passenger pushed a lever forward, the vehicle would start to move.

The hook was attached to a cable like substance and as it moved, it pulled the vehicle. It was steam powered. There are several large paddlewheels placed over the biggest steam vents.

They were capped, except when the forward lever was pushed by the passenger. The cap lifted up, clearing the way for the full force of the vents steam to turn the paddlewheel and pull the transport vehicle.

Rodic arrived at station 87 on level three. Two steam vent tubes were at their maximum output. He knew by those two particular tubes that the El Misti volcano in Peru, was approaching the level of an eruption.

"Get ready to open release tube 14 and I will shut tube number 2. One, Two, THREE."

Each one performed the action Rodic had explained.

"Now I want you to open release tube 15 and I will close tube number 3. One, two, THREE." Once again, they both executed their procedure.

The two pressure tubes for El Misti slowed to a normal and safe output. Rodic replaced the mud caps with new ones.

"Thank you, follower Jong, for your assistance." Rodic said.

With everything at a safe level, Rodic decided to go to his dwelling and be with his family.

Rodic had a wife and two children. His wife, Saren and two small children, Gothy and Basel, which were identical twins.

Things on level two were much better than the other levels. The air was fresher and the entire level was cleaner and the mood of the Gorack's was a happy one.

Rodic entered his home and could smell dinner cooking. His children came running and gave him hugs and his wife gave him a kiss.

"How was your day, honey?" Saren asked.

"Not too much happened. I did avert an eruption in quadrant 23."

"That's a good thing, so don't say not much."

The Gorack's are not aware that there are people that live on the surface. They know nothing by the names we use. Mount Hood is an unknown identity to them. They believe that earth is just that and they're purpose is to protect it from harm.

Their interpretation of harm were volcanic eruptions, earthquakes or anything they deemed a hazarded to earth.

After a fine meal of rodents and cockroaches, Rodic retired for the day.

If it wasn't for the rodents and roaches being able to live underground, food would be a problem. Once in a while a mole or better yet, a groundhog would fall victim to one of the Gorack's traps.

They also had worms, centipedes and a rare variety of red ants, (they were huge in size. Big as two inches in length) for their consumption.

ECUADOR

The bank of Komodo Dragons were only five miles from walking on the beachfront of Ecuador. There had been no progress between the Ecuadorian and American governments on how to resolve the dragon's approach.

President Black had made his decision before any negotiations had begun with Ecuador.

"I can't hope for a resolution from Ecuador. Their too worried about making a wrong decision and it will put them at odds with the voters. I'm going to give the green light on Project Destroy." President Black said.

The President had 12 F-15 jets standing by at one of the eight military bases that the United States has in Peru. For matters of national security, the exact location can't be revealed.

The President called the Peruvian base from the oval office.

"General Wade, green light Project Destroy. Tell the flight commander to make sure the attack kills every single one that represents a threat. There are no limits or restrictions on this mission. Overkill is a must in this mission."

"Yes, Mister President."

The General hung up the phone and gave a thumbs up to the strike's leader.

The 12 jets shot down the runway and headed to the open waters of the Pacific. They arrived in minutes and immediately the pilots saw the large bank of Komodo's nearing land.

They dove one behind the other releasing bombs on the bank. Each jet made four runs over the dragons, dropping a bomb every time. After the 48 passes the waters were a bright red and nothing could be seen moving.

The jets returned to the Peruvian base that they had departed from.

The Ecuadorian President was furious and called President Black.

"What have you done? You have bombed my country, that's an act of war. You will pay for this atrocity!"

"One President to another. You and your officials were so worried about your political life's that you wouldn't make a decision. I know exactly what you wanted. You wanted me to do exactly what I did.

Your going to tell your people the United States attacked them and endangered their life's.

I, in return will show them the footage taken throughout the bombing of the Komodo Dragons. I'll make it clear that you were such a coward, that you were going to allow them to reach land.

Do you think for a minute that voters will be willing to vote for you after you were going to allow these creatures to attack them? No! Mister President. I think your going to be ran out of office for showing your true colors as a coward."

That evening on Ecuadorian television their President praised the United States for their assistance in defeating a deadly attack on the people of Ecuador.

As the Ecuadorian President was speaking, the United States had ground forces on every one of the Galapagos Islands with flame throwers. They were searching for all the egg nests and burning them.

Since Komodo Dragon females can self-fertilize eggs and don't need a male at all for them to reproduce, there are hundreds of nests to be destroyed to stop any newly hatched mutated Komodo's.

ALASKA

The party was in full gear aboard the only cruise ship still operating in the Bearing Sea, when everyone was thrown to the floor. The jolt was so strong that the ship was leaning approximately 14 degrees to the portside.

The guests were screaming and many were tumbling into the Icey waters. The Captain slowly rose from the floor of his bridge to see half the ships crew were either missing or severely injured.

Everyone's first thought was, did they hit an iceberg as the TITANIC had? For a few people out of the 2,045 that were aboard, noticed a huge whale surfacing to breath and then dive.

What made their observation more than relevant was the whale was almost twice the size of the cruise ship they were on. They managed to get to the bridge and informed the Captain of what they had witnessed.

The Captain sent an SOS and a mayday, giving his position and the details of their emergency.

The ship continued to lean more at a slow rate, thank God. By the time the Coast Guard arrived with the only six boats they had and their two helicopters, the ship was leaning in excess of 40 degrees.

No matter how hard people tried to hang on to the elderly and children, some still slipped and drowned in the water.

When everyone that could be rescued, were rescued, the ship was at a 90-degree position when a large wave hit what once was the hulls bottom. The ship rolled over exposing the complete hull and propellers.

It was completely upside down. It was only a few hours after that, that the last part of the ship slowly submerged out of sight under the water.

When it was all over and done. Out of the 2,045 passengers, only 1,218 were accounted for. Out of them, 553 were injured and required medical attention.

Of the 827 dead, only 27 have been recovered. The rest are either still in their cabins or lying on the sea's floor.

The evening news stations around the world showed videos of the rescues and reported on the incident. They had to say that the cause was under investigation; but the governments knew differently.

As far as the people that had witnessed the huge whale, the government came to an agreement with them behind closed doors. No one still to this day know what terms were settled on. However, not one of them has ever said a word about the ship, rescue or what happened.

The whales were a much bigger problem than the Komodo Dragons. The whales couldn't be bombed or shot. They would just dive to extremum depths to elude any threat.

AUSTRALIA

Two professional divers that were shark specialist as well, were hired by the Australian Government to capture one of the mutated sharks. Not only did Dr. Tylor want to study it at the Institute of Oceanography, but also several other agencies for a number of reasons.

Even the cancer research organizations wanted to study it. Since sharks don't get cancer, they wanted to discover why. That study has been going on for many years. The thought was these sharks may hold the answer due to their mutated genealogy.

The Aussie Government had contracted the Anderson Net Company to construct a net made of a light weight material. Its size was to be the size of an American football field, end-zones included.

The net was to be made with Graphene using the method that MIT developed that actually makes it 10 times stronger than before. It's very hard to produce and rare. But there isn't anything the Anderson Net Company can't achieve when they put their brilliant minds to work.

The start date for the Graphene net had started three years prior to the issue of these mutated species. Australia's Minister of Tourism had lobbied for the nets purchase. His reasoning was to control the shark population that was hindering making millions of dollars off Australian tourism.

The net arrived a week ago and the country's involved with the mutated species agreed to rent the net and contribute 25 million each to Australia.

Even though many countries had ordered different types of netting (including Graphene) from the Anderson Net Company, they had just put in their orders within the last six months and were years away from taking possession.

Four large barges pulled a pontoon platform out to the most prominent area where the Great Whites were known to congregate. Once they arrived, the barges came together. Each one had their assigned corner of the net, so they hooked their corner to their barge.

Each pulled away slowly in different directions. The net unfolded and soon it was spread out, lying on the waters surface. A two-hundred-pound weight was then attached to each corner of the net by a large ring.

The two divers dove down to the bottom and drove a steel rod with a ring on its top, two feet into the sandy floor of the ocean.

They were only approximately 185 feet below the surface. They then took a small line that was attached to the ring on the weight above and ran it through the ring on the ocean floor. The end of that line was attached to the corner of the net across from it.

The same was done on the other side as well. The purpose was a well thought out plan with only one foreseeable difficulty.

That was how much the shark would weigh. There was a small possibility it would weigh more than the winches on the barges could control.

The plan was, the crews would through bloody fish carcasses and barrels of fish guts along with blood overboard on top of the net. When the shark came up under the net to reach the bloody feast. The four weights would be pushed off the barges simultaneously.

As the weights sank, the lines the divers had attached to the net's corners would be drawn up to opposite corners, closing the bottom of the net.

The misdirection ring would be dislodged and would be at the bottom of the net so it could be used if need be.

Everything was set, so the signal was given and buckets of dead fish and blood was thrown in the water. In a matter of minutes sonar detected sharks approaching at a fast speed.

It was easy to tell they were sharks by their enormous size. They only wanted one shark. What if two, three or more were participating in the food frenzy? What then?

It was decided that as soon as a shark was in position for the net to enclose him, give the signal.

The second a shark was seen thrashing under the net the signal was given. The weights were pushed off and in seconds the net came together trapping two Great Whites.

One was close to 50 feet and the other close to 62 feet in length. There wasn't a way to truly estimate the weight of the two monsters, but they were being towed easily and the net was holding them in place perfectly.

Josh Hopper was one of the Captains of a barge participating in this government task.

He was aware that the Institute of Oceanography in Hawaii wanted the shark. He had never met Dr. Tylor, but he had an information card that everyone had been given who were working on this project.

He called Dr. Tylor's office only to find out he was in Atlanta, Georgia. He left a message that he wanted to talk to him about the Portuguese-Man-of-War. Everyone had forgotten about the death of his friend by the enormous jellyfish.

ATLANTA CDC

Sarah Winters tapped on the glass door to get Dr. Zurich's attention. She held a note up against the glass and he came over to read it.

He nodded at her and smiled. He turned and approached Dr. Tylor.

"John, Bill Wilson of the State Department, called and said they have a live Great White specimen for you back in Hawaii."

"Wow! Thanks Doc. These are fantastic discoveries that you and your team are isolating. If you will have me, I'd love to came back, but I've got to take delivery of this creature."

"Hell, I understand completely. Go and take care of your business and when your free, come on back. We'll go see a Falcons or Hawks game, depending on what season you're here."

"I will Dr. Zurich. Thank you so much for allowing me to participate in seeing and working in your incredible lab."

Sarah guided Dr. Tylor back to the main lobby once he had disinfected himself and changed clothes.

He was ecstatic in one way, because of the Great White he was receiving and disappointed about leaving the highly secretive CDC lab.

WASHINGTON DC

"Mr. President, Bill Wilson has arrived," said Amy Pierce, the President's assistant.

"Thanks Amy, show him in."

"Good morning Mister President. You wanted to see me sir?"

"Yes, I did Bill. This situation with all these mutated animal attacks seem to be happening more instead of less. The President of Ecuador is fit to be tied. He'll just have to get over it.

The reason I wanted to see you Bill, was I need you to contact all these eggheads that are spearheading what's going on. Call in all the experts and tell them to have there work with them. I want them to prove to me what they can and not a bunch of bull shit.

I'm delighted those entangled in this mess ponied up money immediately and worked with the Australian Government to capture a Great White. Good work, by the way Bill, on overseeing our responsibility in that project.

Don't let anyone of them tell you they haven't the time or can you make it at another time or day. I have this Friday afternoon free from meetings or political functions.

Tell them I personally called this meeting for 1 PM this Friday and it's mandatory, no exceptions. Tell them that and the pervious items I said."

"Yes, Mister President. I'll take care of it immediately."

"Thank you, Bill. Please send Amy in as you leave."

INSTITUTE OF OCEANOGHAPHY

Dr. Tylor was met by David Cornell as he exited the Daniel K. Inouye International airport baggage area.

"Welcome back John. How was Atlanta?"

"Fantastic David. Let me tell you. I'd kill for a lab like Dr. Zurich and his team has. It's more than incredible."

"Your shark arrived about three hours ago and it was delivered to the only place that could accommodate something of that size."

"What's the measurements of it?"

"55 feet long John and 32 feet at it's highest point. What's peculiar is it's calm and shows no aggression."

"That's not what all the reports state from every witness everyone has talked to. Show me where it is. I want to see it for myself."

They got in David's car and he began driving to the far west side of the island.

"Where are we going David? There's nothing this far out that's suitable for something as large as this shark."

"Do you remember when Sea Land Corporation was going to build an amusement park and the biggest aquarium in the world?"

"Yea, but didn't they run out of money and that project has been delayed indefinitely?"

"Yes, but not until after they had constructed part of it and it just so happens, it's the part we need right now."

They arrived at the location that David had found for the sharks' new home.

It was an inlet that was framed in with 20-foot high rock walls and three staggered three to four-foot-thick cement walls. The walls sealed the inlet from the open sea, but allowed the water to come in and out as it normally does.

The developers had dredged the inlet to a depth of 100-feet. The width of the inlet was half a mile wide.

What Dr. Tylor didn't see was the underground facility beneath his feet.

David took him down a flight of stairs and to John's amazement was a 20-foot high by 40-foot long 12-inch-thick plexiglass window.

Dr. Tylor walked up to the glass. He was startled when the huge shark swam right in front of him.

"OMG! That's the biggest creature I've ever seen in its entirety. I saw the whales in Alaska, but nothing like this. How did you find this place? How did you get the owners permission to use it?"

"I called Dr. Thomas Elvan. He's the head of the Presidents new Federal office of Species Migration Patterns. I explain to him the situation and he offered the owners a deal. I'm not privy to that arrangement, but Dr. Elvan called and said the place is ours."

"Great work Dr. Cornell. I appreciate everything you have done here."

At that moment, Dr. Tylor's cell phone rang.

"Hello."

"Dr. Tylor. This is Bill Wilson. The President has schueled a meeting with you and others in the matter of the mutations of animals. You are instructed to bring all data to support your findings."

"I'm very busy, can I reschedule."

"NO! This is mandatory with a no excuse attached to it." With that said, the connection went dead.

WASHINGTON D C

The brilliant minds that were involved with the facing emergency began to arrive at the nations Capital. A few by commercial airlines, but the majority by their private jets.

They congregated at the White House after an intense protocol screening and their verifications. They were led to the conference room, were each had their names on assigned seats. They mingled and introduced themselves to one another.

No need to list all the doctors and individuals that were invited, you know who has been the contributors.

When President Black entered the room, everyone quieted and took their seat.

"Welcome to the White House ladies and gentlemen. It's a pleasure to see that you all made it here today. Not only is the United States facing devastation from these mutated species, the entire world is at risk of suffering the same consequences; if we don't discover a way to stop this from spreading to other species.

My phone is ringing off the hook. The United States is being raked over the coals for killing all the Komodo Dragons. They were on the threatened list. Now they are deemed as endangered or extinctic, depending on who you talk to. I'll discuss that issue with them once we find a solution to the issue facing us at present.

As you see, you were assigned where to be seated. I wanted to hear from each of you on your progress pertaining to this matter. I had you seated in the order I wanted to hear from first, then second and so on.

Captain Troy Bomber, this ordeal started with your submarine being struct. Please start from the beginning and tell me in detail what happened that day. I want to hear about your mission of implanting tracking devices as well."

Captain Bomber began telling his story.

One after the other told what they had learned thus far in detail. The President then asked them to state any hypothesis or theories they had thought of.

It was a long day for everyone. The data from each participant was made available to the others. When everyone was excused and left for home, they had the results from every test dealing with blood, cells, genetics and more.

THE SECREAT
WORLD BELOW

A week had passed since the meeting in Washington D C. There were still attacks being reported; but now they were coming from locations around the world.

Rodic and Saren were sleeping, when they were suddenly being thrown all about. It was the largest earthquake that either of them had ever felt.

Stumbling and falling down, Rodic slowly made his way from level two, to level one.

When he arrived at the PNW station he noticed that area 47 was spewing so much pressure, that it had blown a huge hole in the wall and had destroyed the other tubes.

There was nothing that he or Follower Jong could do. Jong must have been close to the area 47 tube. He was lying on the ground with third degree burns from the steam.

Rodic crawled over to him and pulled him back away from the dangerous steam, in case more of the wall would be blown away.

The shaking continued for over an hour and then as sudden as it had started, it stopped. During the time of the shaking, Rodic tried to help his friend Jong. However, his burns were to severe and he died in Rodic's arms.

Rodic had to leave Jong's side and check on his family. Nothing was functional. Everything had been broken or buried by dirt, rocks or water. Rodic had to move stones and make his way down to the second level anyway he could.

After the long and backbreaking hard work, Rodic made it back to his family. He was pleased to find that both his wife and children were safe and sound.

Saren explained to her husband how she thought they were going to die. She showed him the massive damage done to their home and the blockage of major lava tubes and tunnels. Steam vents had been rerouted and for the first time ever, salt water was being mixed with their fresh water supply.

Rodic felt that he had failed to protect the earth, his family and the Gorack people. He was the leader of the Gorack's and the decision of what to do was his responsibility.

The Gorack had many times suffered cave-ins. The people knew what to do. They didn't need a directive from Rodic to start clearing lava tubes, tunnels and clearing the transporting tubes first.

They worked day and night (by our definition) to return things back to normal. There were concerns about the salt water entering their domain and contaminating the fresh water.

It hadn't slowed entering at all, in fact it was dangerously becoming the dominant water. The temperature was rising as well. Rodic had to make a decision to either stay and hope everything will work out; or search for a new place where the Goracks could live.

One good development about this earthquake was that it was so deep in the earth's core, it wasn't felt on the surface.

It took the Goracks two weeks to reopen their major tubes and the ability to travel to some of the stations. The problem was that the pressure steam tubes for detecting a problem, no longer worked.

Rodic called for everyone to attend a meeting to discuss the situation.

Follower Jong greeted the other Goracks as they entered the meeting area. There were only 200 Goracks and that had been their population for hundreds of years. They kept it at that level as a way to manage their food supply for the future.

As soon as everyone were seated, Rodic addressed the gathering.

"Thank you all for coming. We face a monumental moment in Gorack history. The lava is rising up from its core and is getting closer to our level. The temperature has reached the point that we can't survive here on this level.

Follower Jong found a lava tube that leads upward. How far? I don't know. Will there be fresh water and a suitable temperature for us to exist? I don't know the answer to that either. All I know is that we can't stay where we are.

There's no time to have Follower Jong go on an exploratory fact-finding venture. I feel that we should take as little personal belongings you can and we see where that lava tube leads.

I realize the dangers of it leading nowhere. We must take that chance, because we can't stay here and face certain death.

We can no longer monitor the earth. All of our monitoring steam tubes have been destroyed. I don't know our purpose anymore. We have for hundreds of years controlled the pressure of volcanos and help lowing the devastation from earthquakes.

As every Gorack knows, our history goes back at least a couple thousand years. We don't know how our ancestors became earths guardians or when our first generation was established.

We have our folklore stories about our relatives living on the surface. If we find ourselves on the surface, we'll have to adopt to whatever the situation dictates.

All those that choose to leave by the unexplored lava tube upwards, raise your hands. The majority of the people raised their hand. "All those that choose to stay here and see what happens, hoping it returns to the way it was, raise your hand." Five people, three men and two women.

"I respect each one's opinion and desires. Those that decided to leave, be here tomorrow. You that wanted to stay, I wish you the best and I understand your reason for not leaving your homes."

The next day 195 Goracks stood in front of Rodic's home. He exited his dwelling with his family and Follower Jong.

"It's time for us to begin our journey. Follower Jong, please lead the way to the lava tube." Rodic said.

Jong led the way to the newly discovered lava tube. It was eight feet wide and ten feet tall. The size gave them the room to move freely and not have to crawl or squeeze in between rocks.

The incline got steeper the closer they got to the surface. Since they started their accent more than 25 miles below the surface, they were only able to achieve three to four miles a day.

If it hadn't been for their crude methane gas lights, they would be doing everything in total blackness. Rodic hoped that they would find a big enough cavern that had clean water and livable conditions.

After the fourth day, Rodic and Follower Jong began worrying about the Goracks future. What if the tube came to an abrupt dead end? What if they never found a living space underground? What if at the end of their journey they were standing on earth's surface? What would they see? What if it wasn't livable and was a desolate landscape?

The worrying spread throughout the Goracks as each day they traveled upward without finding a place to call home. One good thing was that fresh water was dripping from the walls. The temperature was cool and that was different for the Goracks, but enjoyable.

Another five days passed without finding a new home. Everyone was exhausted and their food supply had run out two days prior. The stress and anxiety were reaching the point of panic and despair.

THE CDC

Dr. Lance Motto looked up from his microscope with a smile on his face. "Dr. Zurich, come and have a look at this," he said.

He hurried over to see what his colleague had discovered. He looked through the two eye pieces and saw several cells attached to one another. "What am I looking at Lance?"

"That configuration of those six independent cell structures, form a six-cell symbiotic super cell. I had to introduce one cell at a time in the correct order to achieve what you're seeing. I tried thousands of combinations before I succeeded.

The super cell is made up of cells or DNA from oil, cobalt 60, dinosaur DNA, cancer, Orca and Creatine. I have seen many combinations of cells and DNA while studying all over the world.

Working with the information we received at the White House from the other dignitaries, I had a theory and I believe I've discovered a major part of this phenomenon.

The oil that seeps into the ocean naturally is the same amount as we drill and bring to the surface. What is oil? It's dead prehistoric animals (dinosaurs). The DNA, cells and genes are in the oil that's introduced into our oceans.

When you combine the elements from oil with Cobalt-60, (which serves as a radioactive tracer). You produce high energy gamma rays.

Dr. Jill Lamont discovered that combination. She and the other 5 members of my team have all contributed to the super cell's discovery.

I have ascertained that the nuclear meltdown of the Japanese Fukushima Daiichi Nuclear Power Plant, March11, 2011, added radioactive elements at high levels into the ocean. When they came into contact with the seeped oils properties, they bonded together and created the first step of the mutated cells we have now.

Since Dr. Lamont made the discovery, I told her she could name the super cell. She named it, Prealt-1, because elements and DNA's are half prehistoric and half cobalt-60.

We now have to prove how the super cells took over the genetic makeup and became the dominate cellular structure of the different species. It's not easy or even possible to rebuild a DNA's double helix.

I look forward to finding the answer to that mystery. Are there any more questions?"

"No, I think that is more than enough for us to digest at the moment. Great work Dr. Motto. You and your team are beyond phenomenal." Dr. Zurich said.

He returned to his office and called Dr. Erica Jones at THE CELL. He explained what Dr. Motto's team had found and their theory as to how, why and what it meant to them.

Dr. Jones wanted the step by step procedure to duplicate the construction of the super cell Prealt-1.

"I can't give you that even if I wanted to Erica. I don't know it. Only Dr Motto and Dr. Jill Lamont know the correct series of combinations."

"Come on Doc, obtain the needed clearance for me to come to the CDC and have them explain it to me."

"I'll ask Erica, but I know they'll see if you can obtain such a highly security level. At this level, they will overturn every stone from your past. If you have something to hide, tell me now. Do you want me to still ask or forget about it?"

"Please go ahead and ask Doc. I've nothing to hide. I do have a couple of embarrassing things from when I was in college, but hell, who doesn't?"

"Okay Erica. I'll ask Bill Wilson tomorrow and let you know the answer in a few days. It usually takes four or five days to research your background and make the decision."

ALASKA, KODIAK ISLAND

Captain Tome had called Dr. Tylor and informed him of a strange occurrence that was taking place in the Bearing Sea.

Dr. Tylor left Eric Sloan in charge of the Institute of Oceanography's offices so he could return to Kodiak Island.

Captain Tome was waiting as the float plane edged up to the side of the dock. Dr. Tylor stepped out and shook the Captain's hand.

"How are you Dr?"

"I'm doing great," he said sarcastically.

"Yes, I heard you've been on the go for weeks, but I know you would want to hear about this development, ASAP."

"Okay, tell me your big news."

"The whales are dying. There is so many of them, they have eaten everything eatable. There are no more fish, seals, crabs or evidently plankton left for them to feed on. All other foods in their diet are nowhere to be found either.

The squids, sea lions and the sharks that are usually inhabiting our area, all gone. The bigger Killer Whales are turning to cannibalism and eating the smaller of their species."

"Why don't they just go farther out to sea for food?"

"Because they are drawn here by breeding instinct and that drive to return to there home. They are much the same as salmon returning to spawn."

"You are right. I do want to investigate this surprising development."

"Dr. Tylor, this is devastating for this community. The people here make their living by fishing, crabbing and the jobs that facilitate their catch."

"I realize that Captain Tome, but there's nothing I can do to reverse what's happened. I will do whatever I can to help the ecosystem replenish itself as fast as possible."

As the two stood there on the dock, they could hear the whales singing in the distance. As beautiful as the sound was to hear, it also carried economic disaster to Kodiak Island's fishing community. It was sweet and painful with every note they sang.

THE CELL

Dr. Jones, was waiting to hear from Dr. Zurich. She was beside herself in anticipation of obtaining clearance to the secluded lab at the CDC. She wanted to be able to reproduce the Prealt-1 super cell in her lab.

She had a theory of her own and the super cell just might be the missing ingredient to finalize her hypotheses. As she waited for the phone to ring, she went around to each station in the lab, to see where each one was in their assigned task.

CDC

As Dr. Zurich sat in his office going over his many research notes. Dr Jack Lintner from down the hall entered. "Good day Doc. If you've got a minute, I'd like you to have a look at something."

"Sure, Dr. Lintner, what is it?"

"It's an Octopus that just arrived from a colleague of mine that's studying the Great Barrier Reef in Austrailia."

"Jack, I've seen a hundred Octopus in my life."

As they entered Dr. Lintner's lab a large Octopus laid on a table that had been dissected.

"As you can see Doc. Like all Octopus, it has three hearts and nine brains, nothing strange about any of that.

However, the reason I wanted you to come and see this; I heard you were working with mutated cells, genes, etc. Draw the fluid from any one of the hearts and any one of the brains."

The fluid from a heart was a fluorescent orange. The fluid from one of the nine brains was a lime green.

"What the hell is this, Jack?"

"Take both of them back to your lab and look at each sample individually under full magnification using the electron microscope. Then mix the two samples together and have a third look. Have a wonderful day Dr. Zurich," Dr. Lintner said as he walked away.

Needless to say, Dr. Zurich hurried back to his lab. He called Dr. Motto over to assist him and share the findings with him.

After completing the three separate viewings, both men were at a loss for words. They had no idea what they were looking at or what it meant.

Dr. Lintner approached them from behind. "Well, what is it?"

"You tell us Jack. We've no idea, but we sure as hell are going to break it down every way possible to find out. Thank you, for bringing it to my attention. It may indeed have some genetic contribution to Project Discover that we're involved with." Dr. Zurich said.

Suddenly Dr. Zurich's ears perked up as he heard the phone in his office ringing. He literally ran to answer it before it stopped ringing.

"Hello," he said, gasping to catch his breath.

"Hello Doc. I talked to Bill Wilson a moment ago and he talked to his boss. They fast tracked the request upstairs and I was approved almost immediately. I don't know who exactly approved it, but I was.

There are a couple of conditions. I will arrive by an F-15 at Atlanta's Hartsfield-Jackson Airport tomorrow at 9: AM. I can't reveal anything I see or hear, etc. You know the routine."

"Good Erica, I'll see you tomorrow."

Dr. Zurich hung up the receiver and took in a deep breath. He pumped his fist repeatably. He was like a kid in the proverbial candy store. His team had been advancing rapidly in their research. The Prealt-1 super cell would create new theories for his and Erica's team to work on and study.

Dr. Jones tossed and turned that night trying to sleep. She was to wound-up and excited to sleep. When she arrived at the airport the next morning, she parked in the long-term lot, then yawned and shook her head as she walked and entered the terminal.

She knew where to report. Military, government and high priority flights had a special area where the public weren't allowed. She approached the secluded area and was met by an MP.

"Good day Dr. Jones. We were told of your arrival and departure on the waiting F-15. This way doctor, I will escort you to the tarmac, Captain Rodney Brown is prepared to leave as soon as you are aboard." said the MP.

As Dr. Jones climbed into the rear seat, Captain Brown handed her the wraparound glasses she had been advised of. Then a specially designed helmet for such occasions was handed to her and told to put it on as well over the glasses.

"Captain Brown, does this happen very often?"

"Yes, it's the protocol for transporting prisoners to secret locations and even government officials that are allowed to visit restricted areas, but not pareve to their location."

Once Dr. Jones was belted in and was instructed what to do incase of an emergency, the Jet shot down the runway. Dr. Jones's head pushed back into the headrest as the jet's wheels left the runway and Captain Brown put the jet in a sharp angled climb.

True to his word, Dr. Zurich was there to meet Dr. Jones as she climbed down from the jet. She removed the helmet and gave it to Captain Brown. Doc took her hand and walked her into the main Atlanta Airport terminal.

They exited it and got in a white stretch limousine. It didn't take long until they arrived at the CDC. They entered the facility and Dr. Jones stopped. She looked around the huge lobby she was standing in. There were no windows and the glass doors that led into the building were tinted so you couldn't see outside.

"Follow me Erica, I'll introduce you to my team," Dr. Zurich said.

They walked across the lobby and stepped into the elevator against the East wall. Erica noticed that there were no floors above the ground level. Every number on the elevators panel was for a lower level.

Dr. Zurich pushed L-15 and the car started downward.

"Doc, I couldn't help but notice that your choices were LL to L-24. I assume there's only one level above ground." Dr. Jones said.

"Yes, that's correct Erica, but don't worry about that. Well, here we are, level 15 and home to my lab."

Dr. Jones had to go through the same procedure as Dr. Tylor had to when he visited the CDC. Once dressed properly and disinfected, they entered the confines of the biohazard (level 4) lab. Which is the most secure and dangerous environment to work in.

Dr. Zurich introduced Dr. Jones to his team of highly trained experts. The last two individuals she met were Dr. Jill Lamont and Dr. Lance Motto. They were the two that knew more about the Prealt-1 super cell than anyone else.

For the next three hours the four of them constructed a super cell, step by step. Dr. Lamont gave Dr. Jones her notes on the sequence of introductions of each component so that she could reproduce a Prealt-1 super cell for herself in her own lab.

Erica was blown away by the staff working with Doc. There were a few she recognized as being renowned experts in their field from interviews and seminars she had attended. A couple of them she had worked with years prior. She stopped and chatted a few minutes with both of them.

It was time to leave, so the lab technicians could get back to work instead of socializing. Dr Jones thanked her friend Dr. Zurich for the privilege to visit the CDC. They went through the disinfecting chamber, changed back into their clothes and returned to the elevator.

Doc pushed button LL and the car moved upwards. He escorted Dr. Jones to the exit and abide her good-bye.

Once arriving back to the airport, she was escorted to the secured government area. Captain Brown was waiting for her. They had just started walking, when Captain Brown stopped her and reminded her of the wraparound sunglasses. She put them on and he continued to lead her out on to the tarmac.

Dr. Jones made her final jesters and climbed back into the rear seat of the jet. Captain Brown handed her the special helmet and made sure she put it on properly and belted herself securely in place.

Within seconds the jet roared down the runway and went airborne. Dr. Jones wanted to look where she was so badly. She knew if she removed the darken sunglasses, she would never get another clearance to a government facility. She bit her lip and closed her eyes and tried to think about other things to distract herself.

They finally touched down near Dr. Jones's secret facility, THE CELL, as the sun was just starting to disappearing below the horizon.

She took one of the shuttle buses to the long-term lot and retrieved her car. She paid the attendant and the gate's arm raised for her to exit the lot.

She was more than tired or bushed. She was wiped out beyond words. Once home, she walked in the house and went straight to the bedroom and fell spread eagled across the bed, clothes and all. She must have been asleep before actually hit the mattress, because she was snoring a split second before hitting it.

She had learned a lot of valuable data and acquired important facts about genetics, genealogy and cellular construction.

She had wondered why Dr. Tylor gained entry to the CDC without being vetted, but she had been. She learned that he was the Director of Project Discover. His job was cleared to gather information from every facility and person involved with the project.

She had also been told by Captain Brown on the flight home, the reason for the wraparound sunglasses being so dark that you couldn't see anything, was so that the control panel couldn't be seen or memorized by anyone. Even Senators and Congressmen had to wear the same sunglasses.

THE DECEPTIVE

The repairs were finally finished on the Deceptive and it was ordered to go out on a test run to verify its performance. It was flanked by a Cyclone class patrol ship during its maneuvers. If there were to be a problem, the USA couldn't leave an Ohio class nuclear submarine unattended.

The sub went through its maneuvers and Captain Bomber pushed each one to the limit. He had to be 100% sure that he could trust his ship. He was responsible for the life of each of the crew. When you're submerged 2 or 3 hundred feet deep, there's not much to do if you have a major incident.

Finally, Captain Bomber was satisfied that he could trust the Deceptive under any conditions. He returned to the docking area and dismissed the crew.

The Deceptive was fit and ready for any duty that would come its way.

AUSTRALIA

Reports were coming across the major news outlets that dead sharks were washing up on Australian beaches. Not only that, they were enormous in size.

That was baffling to much of the public, but government officials and the science community knew of mutated sharks.

Dr. Tylor was contacted by and directed to investigate the strange events that were occurring there. He was glad to be leaving the cold in Alaska for the warm Australian weather.

It was a long flight and the one-hour break to refuel and eat while in Honolulu, was a true blessing. He finally arrived in Sydney and Josh Hopper was waiting for him as he exited the ramp to the terminal.

"Great to see you again Dr. Tylor," Josh said.

"It's great to be back and enjoy your wonderful weather," he said.

"I've got a car waiting to take us to the marina. We've only a couple of hours of daylight and I wanted you to see this as fast as possible." Josh stated.

It was a short drive to Josh's boat. They boarded the craft and Josh fired up the twin inboard motors. He backed out of the slip slowly and then pushed the throttle to its maximum position. The boat shot out of the harbor, ignoring the no wake and speed limit signs that were posted.

He knew there would be a heavy fine waiting for him upon his return. In the back of his mind, he was hoping Dr. Tylor with is government pull, could talk the harbormaster out of writing him one.

Dr. Tylor was astounded by what he was viewing with his own eyes. Countless bodies of Great White sharks all along the beautiful Australian beaches. He noticed one particular thing that was unusual. A few of the dead sharks had a jellyfish attached to them.

The jellyfish were 90 percent of the Box jellyfish variety, but there were one or two Portuguese Man of War jellyfish too. Dr. Tylor knew that a box jellyfish can sting a shark and kill it with no question. The Portuguese man of War has to be a bigger than normal one, but it can kill a shark if big enough.

John draw several blood samples from at least a dozen sharks and cut out a 12-inch square of flesh around the major sting area. He photographed the site and made videos showing the enormity of the shark deaths.

He immediately called Dr Jones at THE CELL and sent her the pictures and video he had taken. He was standing on the beach when she told him to put the samples on a F-15 ASAP and send them to her.

"Captain Brown is on his way to Honolulu as we speak. Thomas Elvan, the head of the Species Migration Patterns (SMP) was thinking ahead about samples. He ordered Captain Brown to Hawaii hours ago. It's nice to have someone in Washington who takes care of business." Erica said.

"I'm on my way to the airport right now. Thanks Dr. Jones."

Josh started the motors and they returned to the harbor. As he had surmised, the harbormaster was standing on the dock with a Coast Guard Officer.

"OH crap. I'm about to get chewed out and pay for the privilege." Josh said.

"Mister Hopper, a word please," said the harbormaster.

"Good evening gentlemen. I'm Dr. John Tylor and I'm the head of a government highly secured project. I know we departed the harbor in a less than appropriate manner, but time was essential and I told Mr. Hopper to ignore the harbors protocol. I assure you it was a matter of great importance that we left in said manner. Please, don't punish Josh for my orders to speed away as fast as possible."

"Dr. Tylor. Are you the one that's been up in Alaska?" said the Coast Guard Officer.

"Yes, I just left there to come here."

"My friend Captain Tome was telling me about you today. I understand the work your involved with. Mr. Hopper, consider this a verbal warning and both of you have a nice day," he said.

Josh drove Dr. Tylor to the airport and after showing the proper ID he was allowed access to the secured area. He met Captain Brown and handed over the samples. In a matter of seconds, he watched as the F-15 roared down the runway and disappear into the night.

With his main business completed, Dr. Jones took it upon himself to pay for a commercial flight back to Hawaii. He didn't want to waste time having another F-15 come and retrieve him. He just wanted to go home and relax.

WASHINGTON DC

It was a media frenzy as the Presidents of Ecuador, Peru and Columbia arrived at the White House. President Black met each one as they exited their vehicles. They were there for an important meeting concerning the future of the Komodo Dragon being reintroduced back in the Galapagos Island Chain.

President Black wanted this meeting held behind closed doors with no press present. He had however, invited Dr. Igor Botanic, the world's leading authority on reptilian reproduction and their genetic DNA abilities.

The five of the them gathered in the Oval Office and after they had been served coffee and the servers had left, President Black opened the conversation.

"Welcome President Gomez, President Garcia and President Sanchez to the White House. Thank you, Dr. Botanic for coming as well. Gentlemen, this is Dr. Igor Botanic, the best mind in the field of reptiles.

He will answer your questions on repopulating the Komodo Dragons back to their island homes."

"How do you believe that can be accomplished?" President Gomez asked.

"I was in Puerto Villamil last week, studying soil samples to make sure it was still adequate for them to return. I concluded that it is and that's a major huddle cleared.

Komodo Dragons are rare once you ignore the Galapagos Island Chain. There're very few zoos that even try to breed or raise them. I however, have a few connections that have access to half a dozen breeding pairs.

At the moment, I have six eggs in an incubator in my research lab in Austria. When they hatch and I feel there're healthy enough to survive on their own. I will release them on the biggest Galapagos Island. I will stay and monitor their adjustment to their new surroundings, no pun intended." Dr. Botanic said.

That evidently was all it took to satisfy the three Presidents from South America on replenishing the dead Komodo's.

Dr. Botanic was excused and for the next four hours the atmosphere changed to a much less friendly one. It was one of the USA not having or asking for actions that it took on several fronts. It took some compromising form President Black to smooth over the actions that had taken place on foreign soil, airspace and diplomacy.

Thankfully, the issue came to an acceptable conclusion for everyone in the Oval Office. They all had a delicious dinner in the White House dining room. The four wives got along splendidly and the men talked politics relating to the Middle East and Russia.

The evening ended with laughter and hardy handshakes as the three foreign Presidents and their wives returned to their hotels.

INSTITUTE OF
OCEANOGRAPH

Dr. Tylor collected his go-bag from the airport's carousel and approached what is affectionally called, taxi alley. He spotted his favorite cab driver, Jose Ramarao and flagged him to the curbside.

"Hello, Dr. Tylor, welcome home. Where would you like to go tonight, your lab or straight home?" Jose asked.

"I wanted to go straight home, but I got a text stating someone is at the lab waiting for me. I guess I'll go there first Jose."

"Yes sir, Dr. Tylor." Jose said.

John settled into the backseat and closed his eyes. It would only take a few minutes to arrive at the Institute, but a few minutes relaxing was better than none.

Eventually the cab pulled up to the main entrance of the Institute. John paid Jose as well as a good size tip before the taxi sped away.

Dr. Tylor entered the front lobby and was immediately met by a tall, slender well-tanned individual.

"Good afternoon Dr. Tylor. I am Dr. Nick Brownstone. I have been advised to render my services to Project Discover by the director of the SMP, Dr. Thomas Elvan. I have lived on Guadalupe Island for almost 30 years.

I am the expert on the biggest Great White ever recorded and viewed. Deep Blue is her referred name by everyone in the field of shark studies. She is 22 feet in length, 10 feet across and estimated to weigh over three-tons.

There is a place off the coastline of Guadalupe Island called The Ledge. Its over 1000 feet deep and is home for her and other mega-sharks. She has not been seen at The Ledge for six years.

She's over 50 years old and has given birth to dozens of pups. The reason I came 3000 miles to Hawaii is she was spotted here a week ago and is impregnated again.

The appearance of mega sharks has been developing over the last twenty years, Sharks that are 18,19, 20 plus in length are becoming the norm.

I am here to work with you and Project Discover. We need to compare blood samples, tissue analyzes and DNA genetics to see if this tremendous jump from 20 feet to over 50 feet, is connected to the mega sharks I am researching at present.

We need to know if the sharks your Project Discover are involved with have a different origin than the genetic code I am working with.

I was instructed that I have total clearance to the CDC and anywhere I need, except for a facility named THE CELL."

"That's educational for sure Dr. Brownstone. I have indeed heard of your research and Deep Blue. She is more famous than the shark in the movie Jaws. I had committed myself to contact you once my project either came to a conclusion or ran aground.

I'll call Bill Wilson at the State Department and have Captain Brown fly you to the CDC tomorrow morning. Ninety-nine percent of our traveling is done with Captain Brown in a F-15.

Do you have a place to stay Dr Brownstone?"

"Yes, I'm checked in at the Honolulu Hilton and my luggage has already been delivered to my room."

"That's fine, I'll call a taxi to take you to your hotel."

Dr. Tylor called the cab company and asked for Jose especially and he returned to the Institute almost immediately.

"Jose, this is my friend. Treat him as if it were me and take him to the Honolulu Hilton."

"Yes, Dr. Tylor." Jose said in return.

John wanted to go home and relax, but now he decided to once again sleep in his office's small rest area there at the Institute.

He called Bill Wilson and Dr. Zurich. He set in motion Dr. Brownstone's travel arrangement and gave Dr. Zurich a head ups that Dr. Brownstone was coming.

Finally, he made it to bed and drifted into a deep sleep.

HISTORY OF THE SECREAT WORLDS HABITANTS

As Rodic and the Goracks struggled upwards, they came to an abrupt stop. They could see a dim light off in the distance lighting the lava vent ahead.

"We have to stop for now. We have to investigate the strange light that lies ahead before we continue," Rodic said.

"I will go and see what lies ahead Rodic," Follower Jong said.

"Rest for a while Jong. After a well-deserved sleep, you can go," Rodic advised him.

"Yes, thank you Rodic."

The rumors of the Goracks once living on the surface was correct. Hundreds and hundreds of years ago they called the surface world their home. They lived among the dinosaurs and the dangers in the world back then.

Earthquakes and repeated volcano eruptions were an everyday occurrence. The Goracks made sacrifices to the gods they believed in.

When a Gorack would die from an attack or from being sick, their body was offered to the lava god and tossed into the fiery pit of a volcano. Once a year, when the first bud had bloomed on the village fruit tree a live virgin was sacrificed.

They believed that would appease the gods and spare them from the wrath they could level against them. As the years passed and the earthquakes and eruptions grew in size and frequency, fear spread across the faces of the Goracks.

The methane gas was so strong that infants and the old were vomiting and many were dying. The sun was to the point of being nonexistent. The heavy smoke and ash covered the sky day and night.

When it became obvious to the Goracks that they could no longer survive where they were. They retreated to the inner earth for protection from the polluted air and the increasing number of dinosaurs.

The water was polluted and the air bad at first, but as they continued downward the environment got better. After days of seeking a home, they came across a cavern that was big enough for the Goracks to live.

The air was clean and the water was pure and cool. The Goracks have lived in that location over the years. It's the exact place where Rodic and the Goracks were living before they were forced to seek a new home.

Rodic, had no idea what laid ahead for him and the Goracks. He knew they had to find a place fast. They were out of food and water. Many were weak and were close to not being able to continue the search.

After his time sleeping, Follower Jong shook Rodic's hand and continued upwards to see if the Goracks would be safe continuing.

The closer he got to the light, the brighter it became. It hurt his eyes to look further up the lava tube. He had to stop his ascent; he was afraid to get closer to the light. He knew the Goracks were counting on him to report his findings one way or the other.

He sat there debating with himself about what he should do. A few hours passed and the light began to fade in brightness until it no longer was visible. He got to his feet and hurried up the vent.

It took him an hour to reach the end of the vent. He stepped out of it and for the first time saw the stars and moon high above in the sky. He was amazed and mesmerized as he witnessed a shooting star streak across the sky.

He stood like a statue while focusing on the twinkling of stars, he couldn't pull himself away from the heavenly display.

The wonderful view began to fade as the sun started to rise. Jong felt the warm rays of the sun as they lit his face. He entered the lava tube and as the light got brighter, he felt it on his back, so he continued back to where he had spent his time earlier.

He rested a minute and then proceeded downward to reunite with Rodic and the Gorack people.

He finally reached Rodic and everyone tried to get close enough to hear what Jong had discovered.

"I can't explain why, but it is dark and beautiful for several hours. Then it becomes brighter than I have ever seen and the light burned my eyes and skin. We could live easily when it's dark. It's cool and a large ball of light glows high above. It didn't harm me at all.

I didn't see any water or food because it was dark. I suggest Rodic, that we proceed upward to the end of the lava tube. We have enough parcels to close the opening and block the light when necessary. Then we can explore in the dark for water and food." Jong said

"We have to do something. We can't go back and we can't stay here. We must find water and food or we'll all die in a few days. Let's move forward everyone. Gather your belongings and follow Jong and me upwards." Rodic stated.

It took several hours for the Goracks to reach the opening to the surface world. The light was just starting to appear. Everyone handed their bags and belongings forward in a fireman bucket relay. It only took a few seconds before the opening was sealed from letting the light enter.

It was time to rest and sleep. Everyone including Rodic were weak and quickly becoming dehydrated. Rodic knew he and Pang would have to venture out into the light in search of water and food, the survival of the Gorack people depended on it.

As the light started to diminish, Jong removed several bags from the opening. He and Rodic exited the lava tube and ventured out into this new world with great suspicion.

They could see fine in the dusk lit surroundings. They were standing in the middle of a forest. They didn't know what trees were or what it meant that hundreds were standing in the same area They were startled when a buck and three does walked across their path about sixty yards in front of them.

"Food!" They both said in unison.

They continued searching by the light from a full moon. Suddenly, they discovered a stream with clean water flowing freely. Their eyes opened wide and a smile from ear to ear spread across their faces.

They had found a new home. There was food, water and shelter. The Goracks could sleep in the lava tube while they built structures from the wood. The Goracks were highly inventive and had built their elaborate transportation system and pressure monitoring tubes that they controlled volcanic eruptions with.

They headed back to the lava tube with several bags of water. The had brought the bags along for just this purpose if they found water.

They were a welcome sight for the Goracks as the water bags were passed around by the people. Everyone only got a sip; but the news of there being plenty of water put new hope and energy in everyone.

The Goracks held a meeting to come up with a plan for them to adjust to the bright light. The only solution was to cover up their bodies so they wouldn't burn their skin and shade their eyes. They were convinced that over time they would adjust to their new surroundings and environment.

The decision was made that all the Goracks would exit the lava tube when the light started to dim. They would gather water and some of the men would hunt for food.

It was the perfect night for the Goracks to have a successful night. All the water they needed was collected and taken back to the tube for safe keeping.

The men that had went hunting were excellent in their technique. Those hundreds of years trapping and capturing rats, moles and other varmints was paying off.

They knew how to be up wind, stalk and have patience. In their previous home they did the same approach and used a spear to stab their prey.

The only thing different was a much larger spear. By the end of the night they had killed three dear and one bull elk. It was a joyful feast for the Goracks that night.

The sun began to rise and the light slowly started moving across the landscape towards them. The Goracks that had stuffed themselves to the point of being in pain, hurried as fast as they could to retreat back inside the lava tube.

The last one of the Goracks (Rodic) restacked the bags and sealed the entrance for their safety.

The stench for the Goracks urinating and defecating was overwhelming. Even though they were going a hundred yards back down the lava tube to relieve themselves.

At their previous home they did these bodily functions in the underground river. The waste simply floated away downstream and away from their living quarters.

Rodic made the decision that when darkness returned, they would shelter under the shade from the trees during the light's presence. They would have to shield their eyes and hope eventually they would adjust.

The Gorack's had another issue to deal with. One of their elders had passed away during their feast of dear and elk. At the moment the body was covered with leaves and limbs under a large pine tree.

They had always made their deceased a sacrifice, but there weren't active volcanos here for them to carry out that tradition.

Rodic assembled the highest ranking Goracks to discuss how to deal with the issue of their deaths from this point on.

Finally, a decision was unanimously agreed on. The Goracks came from the underground of earth. It was only fitting that the dead be returned to the earths underground. They would bury their dead in the same manner we bury our love ones.

As the light faded, the Goracks exited the lava tube with all their belongings. They went into the forest and built lean twos and gathered branches for more protection.

When the sun began to rise, the Goracks had built over 150 shelters. Each had adequate water supply and food for two days. The hunters had to go hunting for food the next night before their food supply was gone.

THE CDC

Captain Brown touched the wheels of the F-15 down smoothly on the runway at Atlanta's International Airport. He taxied to the restricted area for governmental and classified arrivals and departures.

As Dr. Brownstone exited the jet, he handed the helmet and wraparound sunglasses back to Captain Brown.

Sarah Winters was waiting to meet Dr. Brownstone when he arrived.

"Dr. Brownstone, I'm Sarah Winters from the CDC. My official title is hostess or greeter, whichever you like. I see to the needs of all visitors to the CDC facility.

There's no need to check into a hotel, there are wonderful accommodations at the CDC facility. Follow me Dr. and I'll introduced you to Dr. Zurich, he's expecting you."

"Thank you, Miss Winters. I'm looking forward to meeting Dr. Zurich and viewing the CDC facility."

They exited the terminal and entered the Classic Limousine that Brent Smith had waiting for them. It didn't take long for them to arrive at the CDC facility.

Sarah showed Dr. Brownstone to his room. He put his one small bag on the bed and continued with Sarah to the elevator. Down it went and then came to an abrupt stop at level 15.

Dr. Jack Lintner met Dr. Brownstone when he stepped out of the elevator.

"Welcome to the CDC and Dr. Zurich's level 4 laboratory. I'll show you the mandatory procedure to enter the lab."

Dr. Brownstone had to go through the same disinfection chamber and dress codes like others had before him. Once he had completed the necessary requirements, he was allowed to enter the actual lab.

"Welcome Dr. Brownstone to my lab, I'm Dr. Zurich and Dr. Tylor notified me of your arrival. I have been watching your reports and findings of mega sharks and especially Deep Blue. She's a monumental research specimen.

I am excited to compare her blood sample results with the blood that Project Discover have from these mysterious mutated sharks."

"I notified my office on Guadalupe Island to send an overnight delivery to the CDC last night. I checked the tracking number while riding in the limo and it should be arriving any minute."

"That sounds good, I can hardly wait to view those blood samples under full magnification of the electron microscope."

"I can't either Dr. Zurich. I don't have an electron microscope at my disposal. I can only increase 50,000 X. It may show both of us something we have never seen."

Suddenly there was tapping on the glass coming from Sarah holding a package that was labeled caution, bio-hazard. It was a Styrofoam cube approximately 18 by 18 inches.

"That's my samples Dr. Zurich. There're packed in a coolant to keep them stabilized while in transit."

Dr. Lintner went and retrieved the package and brought it to Dr. Brownstone.

He opened it and revealed several tubes of blood and four pieces of flesh.

"These blood samples are from Deep Blue when she is impregnated and when she isn't. The four pieces of 3-inch square flesh is from her as well"

"Let's put a blood sample under the electron microscope. It's killing me, Dr. Brownstone, to see the results."

Dr. Jill Lamont took one of the tubes of blood and put a sample in the labs centrifuge. As that sample was spinning, Dr. Zurich placed a slide under the electron microscope.

He focused the image at the highest magnification he could achieve until it was crystal clear for his inspection.

"OMG! I can't believe what I'm looking at. Look at this Dr. Brownstone and tell me what you see."

"Bacteria and a virus? The two are merging together making a mutated cellular entity that's multiplying and that's impossible. It goes beyond believability and goes against all fundamental laws of physics.

A bacteria and a virus can exist in the blood stream independently from one another. However, they can't bond together, creating a new mutated cell.

How is it possible that the two can successfully accept one another?"

"We've been looking at this horrendous mutation of different spices the wrong way. We've been studying Viruses and their effect on cellular construction to alter DNA's double Helix.

This defiantly shows bacteria is one of the main components to the mutations of cells and DNA. I have to call Dr. Erica Jones at The Cell and make her aware of this development." Dr Zurich said.

Now that bacteria's had become a component in the birth of mutated cells affecting the sea life and reptilians, the parameters had increased ten-fold.

Dr. Zurich called Dr. Jones and explained to her the discovery they had with the blood sample from Deep Blue.

"I know Dr. Brownstone's work with Deep Blue. I even went to one of his lectures at the University of Hawaii three years ago. It was very interesting and informative. I introduced myself to him afterwards; but he probably doesn't remember me." Dr. Jones said.

"I'll send you a sample of Deep Blue's blood for your inspection and testing."

"I have a better idea Doc. Tell Dr. Brownstone that I'll obtain the clearance for him to visit me at The Cell. He can bring a sample himself," Erica said.

"That sounds great Erica. I'll relay your message to him, I'm sure he will be ecstatic. He's in the disinfection chamber at the moment. We're going to dinner and mull over how we should move forward."

"I'll get back to you with the when and travel arrangements ASAP."

"Thanks Erica, have a good night," Doc said as he hung up the phone.

He made his way to the disinfection chamber and then met Dr. Brownstone in the CDC lobby. They exited the facility and Brent Smith opened the limo's door for them.

"Where to Dr. Zurich?" Brent asked.

"Take us to The Seaworthy Ahoy, Brent."

"Very nice Restaurant sir. You always have wonderful taste." Brent replied.

THE GORACKS

It took roughly two weeks for the Goracks to adjust to the sun's light. They had also covered up and only mildly suffered sunburns. Food was plentiful and abundant fresh clean water made their new world more than satisfactory.

One day Rodic heard a loud bang noise that startled him. He shrugged it off, but later the same day he heard the sound again, only closer.

He was worried because he didn't know what it could be. He was concerned if it was something friendly or dangerous. As leader of the Goracks, it was his responsibility to protect each and every one of the Goracks.

Rodic signaled for Follower Jong to come over to him. They each took the spears they had made for hunting and went off in the direction of the loud bang Rodic heard.

"We must stalk what ever it is that we seek." Rodic said.

Another bang sounded and this one was much louder and so close that the two fell to the ground and looked around. They didn't want to move unless whatever it was would see them.

After a few minutes Rodic heard voices approaching to where they had taken up refuge.

A moment later two men came visibly carrying an apparent dead buck. It was great that their language was the same as the Goracks (English).

Rodic's curiosity got the best of him. He waned to know where the Goracks were and was there others like him. Rodic stood up and loudly said, "Hello."

The two men waved, smiled. One of the men asked, "Having any luck?"

Seeing they were friendly, Rodic walked up to them and offered his hand to them. They both shook his hand and offered him a beer. Rodic had no idea what beer was, but if they were drinking it, he might as well.

Rodic motioned for Follower Jong to come and join them. Jong joined them and the two men shook his hand and gave him a beer as well.

"I'm Rodic and this is Jong, my friend."

"I'm Joe and this is Bob. I can't help but notice you only have a spear. Is that what you hunt dear with?" Joe asked.

"Yes, it serves us well." Rodic said.

"Why don't you use a gun like this Winchester 30/30?" Bob asked.

"What is a gun? How does it work?"

"You don't know what a gun is? Where are you from Rodic?" Bob questioned.

"I come from the earth, but I don't know about guns. How does it work?"

"Show him Joe."

"Okay, this is a bullet and it goes right in here. Then you look through this eyepiece called a scope. When you see what you want to shoot, you just slowly pull this thing here called the trigger."

Joe pulled the trigger and Rodic discovered where the loud sound had come from. He also saw a large piece of bark explode off a tree many yards away from him.

"You want to give it a try Rodic?" Bob asked.

"Okay, I'd like that very much."

Bob handed his rifle to Rodic and helped him in how to hold and sight something through the scope.

Rodic had picked out a tree approximately a hundred yards away. When the crosshairs were exactly where Rodic wanted to shoot, he slowly squeezed the trigger. When the bark exploded off the tree he was aiming at, he was mesmerized.

"I have got to have a gun. It's much better than a spear."

Bob and Joe laughed and told him that a gun was a whole lot better than a spear.

"Where can I get one."

"There's several place in town you can get one." Joe said.

"Town?"

"Yea, Klamath Falls. Your only twenty miles from there. You know you're in Oregon, right?" Bob asked.

Rodic didn't want to sound stupid so he said "Yes, I just though you meant a different town."

"Nice to have met you guys, but we got to get going. It's a long way back to our truck and nightfall is closing in fast." Joe said.

"Thank you, Bob and Joe." Rodic said as the two walked away carrying their shot dear.

"Their right Rodic. Let's get back to our people." Pang said.

THE CELL

Captain Brown put the wheels down and the F-15 screeched as its tires touched the runway of the secret location of The Cell.

Dr. Brownstone again handed Captain Brown the helmet and wraparound sunglasses after exiting the jet.

Dr. Erica Jones met him personally there on the staging area of the runway. She wasn't concerned about Dr. Brownstone figuring out where he was. He had spent thirty years on an island and hadn't been in the United States for forty-two years.

"It's an honor to finally met you Dr. Brownstone. I have followed your work for many years. I have been curious about Deep Blue for years myself. She's definitely one of a kind. I look forward to studying her bloods results."

"Thank you, Dr. Jones. I remember you from my seminar in Hawaii a few years back. You approached me after I had addressed the students on shark behavior and their tendencies."

"You're right, I did indeed seek you out after your informative lecture. Come with me, I want you to see my lab and get to work comparing our samples."

They walked a little less than a hundred yards and entered the government facility. They entered the one and only elevator. A security guard with Dr Jones's protection party pushed the button LL on the elevators panel.

The car descended rapidly, giving Dr. Brownstone a queasy stomach. He was relieved when the ride finally came to a stop.

"Here we are Dr. Brownstone. As you may have noticed, there were no numbers on the panel or lit numbers showing how deep we traveled. I can tell you that my level 4 lab is 287 feet below the surface.

We house the same deadliest bacteria's and virus's known to mankind that the CDC have. They aren't secluded or hid away from the public. It's almost impossible for anyone to break in and steal them. The key word is almost and that's the reason for The Cells existence.

We have our protective procedure at CDC before obtain entry into the lab." Dr. Jones said.

Once complying with the safety precautions, they entered the level 4 lab. Dr. Brownstone opened a small box he had been carrying and revealed 6 vials of Deep Blue's blood samples. He turned and handed the box to Erica. She in return handed five of the vials to her lab technicians and kept one for herself.

"Let's see what we have to compare with my samples."

Erica smeared a small amount on a slide and placed it under her lab's electron microscope.

"WHOA! What in hell's happening? I couldn't believe it when Doc called and explained his labs findings. Let's review what's taken place here.

We have a virus that's in the form of a microscopic (virion) bonding with bacteria in a (Cell) form. The unbelievable issue is that the two are creating a new super cell, twice the size of the bacteria's original cell.

The new super cell according to Dr. Jill Lamont at the CDC states that it's not related to either the cell or virion that created it. It has its own DNA and it's a cell related to nothing but itself. It's a new life form and she has no idea what it's limitations might me.

I got an update from Doc a few minutes before you landed Dr. Brownstone. We may have found something more important and dangerous than large mammals and animals.

Everybody, breaking down this super cell's DNA and every molecule, genetics, neutrons, electrons and protons. You get the picture; we have to dissect this super cell to the point we understand its full potential. Get to work everyone," she said.

THE GORACKS

Everything was going smoothly as the Goracks were fishing and gathering wood to cook the fresh meat that the hunters had just returned with. They were surprised when six men walked in to their domain.

"Hoody folks, I'm game Warden Van Green and these men are my deputies. I had a report of a large group of people living in the woods they were hunting and fishing. I would like to see your fishing and deer hunting licenses or any other tags you might have in your procession.

That's a mighty fine six point you got hanging over there and that's a beautiful German brown trout being filleted," warden Green said.

"I wasn't aware we need something in order to fish or hunt." Rodic said.

"Yes sir, you have to purchase a license in order to hunt or fish. If you don't have one, I have to confiscate your deer and fish. I also have to write you a ticket for both infractions. Do you understand what I'm saying completely or would you like more information?"

"What's a ticket and where can I find this place to get a license?"

"Go to the sporting goods store in town. They will be happy to sell you everything you need to be in accordance with the law."

"Sell, as in buy?"

"yes sir, tell the salesman what you need and give him the money and you're good to go."

"What is money?"

"Okay mister, let me see some ID, no one likes a joker or comedian."

"I don't have anything that says I'm Rodic. We have never had to prove who we were, we all know one another."

"What's your full name?"

"Rodic, that's all it is. We only have one name and mine is Rodic."

"You mean to tell me that all these people have no ID and only have one name?"

"Yes, that's correct. I'm sorry if we have broken any of your laws, but we didn't know."

"Where are you folks from?"

"From the earth."

"That's what a couple of hunters said you told them the other day."

"Oh, you mean Joe and Bob. They were nice guys. I enjoyed talking with them."

"Rodic, where exactly did you and all these people come from and don't say from the earth?"

"But that's the truth Warden Green. My people have lived below the surface for hundreds of years. We have been forced to relocate to the surface due to the recent earthquakes and volcanic eruptions."

"I've heard enough. Mr. Rodic or whatever your name really is, come with me. I'm taken you to the ranger station and decide what to do with you and your people. You're all squatting on BLM property and that's against the law as well."

"Isn't there anything that's not against your law?"

"Don't be a smart-ass Mr. Rodic. Come on guys, lets go back to the station."

"I'll be back soon, until then Follower Jong is leader of the Goracks." Rodic said as he smiled at his wife and children.

THE CELL

Dr Erica Jones was totally surprised when she saw a man tapping on the glass of her level 4 lab. She didn't recognize him, but she did recognize the Vice President of the United States, Richard Morehouse.

She walked over to the glass and pushed the button on the intercom system.

"Hello, Mister Vice President. What has brought you here to my lab sir?"

"This is Dr. Igor Botanic from Austria. The President wants him on Project Discover as a co-leader with you. He's the world's greatest authority on reptilian DNA, cellular construction, genetics and reproduction. It's important that we discover how a female Komodo Dragon doesn't need a male to become impregnated. He also just hatched six Komodo eggs and has samples to compare."

"Thank you, Mister Vice President. I'll send Dr. Mote out to walk Dr. Botanic through the labs procedure to enter."

"Thank you, Dr. Jones, and don't take this personally. The president feels two brilliant minds are better than one and in no way is this a reflection on your abilities," the Vice President said.

Dr. Mote walked Dr Botanic through the protocols and then escorted him into the level 4 lab.

THE GORACKS

Warden Green led Rodic through the woods to the ranger station. Warden Green had radioed ahead to the Sheriff's Office about the unusual predicament he found himself in and was requesting backup.

By the time Rodic and the game officers reached the ranger station, the Sheriff was already waiting for them.

"This is the man you were talking about Van?"

"Yes, it is Officer Watts."

"I'm Officer Rich Watts with the Sheriff's Department. Van tells me you've been hunting and fishing without proper documentation and you're squatting on BLM land. What do you have to say about all that?"

"I didn't know I needed permission to live, fish and hunt. As I told Warden Green, I'm sorry and we will move and not hunt or fish any longer."

"I'm afraid it's not that easy. You and your friends have no ID's and won't reveal where you originated from."

"I already told Warden Green we all came from the earth, below the surface to be more precise."

"Okay mister Rodic, I'm taking you to Bellevue for evaluation. Please come with me. I have to lock you up for your and my protection."

Rodic was frightened for the first time being on the surface. He had never been restricted and he didn't understand why he was not going back to his family.

Once they arrived at the Bellevue Institute, Rodic was admitted for evaluation. It was the first time that he saw a city. He was amazed by the tall buildings and especially the colored lights all over the city.

The feeling abruptly disappeared when a phlebotomist stuck a needle in his arm and drew blood from it. His mind was full of wild visions to what these people were going to do to him. He tried to fight off the desire to panic, but he couldn't. As he was struggling to free himself, he was stuck with another needle and he almost immediately fell asleep.

It didn't take long for the results from Rodic's blood work to show an astounding fact. His blood was made up of only a large mutated cell. His results being strange and out of the ordinary was cause for alarm.

The CDC was notified immediately by the Bellevue Institute's Director Ben Snow. He explained their concern for the issue at hand. Dr. Zurich was contacted by his Director and informed that a sample was in transit to the CDC.

When Rodic became coherent, he saw a man in a white smock staring at him.

"What do you want from me?" Rodic asked.

I'm Dr. Jim Wheeler, I'm Bellevue's Institutes on staff psychiatrist and I'd like to ask you a few questions. Are you up to having me do that right now?"

"Sure, ask me anything. I just want to go back to my people. Can I do that after I talk to you?"

"We'll see. You said your name is Rodic and that's your entire name correct?"

"Yes."

"You came from where you were living underground to the surface, because of the recent earthquakes and volcanic eruptions, correct?"

"Yes, I've been over this time and time again. I want to go back to my people now."

Dr. Wheeler could see that Rodic was getting more upset and was on the edge of becoming belligerent; so, he orders a sedative for Rodic and watched as he slipped back into a deep sleep.

"I don't think he knows he's only a couple of miles from Crater Lake." Dr. Wheeler said as he left the room with nurse Amy Baker.

THE CDC

Dr. Zurich was elated when he took procession of the blood samples from Bellevue Institute. He called across the lab for Dr's Motto and Lamont to assist him in what he was going to view.

Dr. Zurich opened the package and broke the seal on one of the tubes containing Rodic's blood. He placed some blood on a slide and slid it under the microscope.

"Oh my God! This blood consists of only super cells. Do you understand what this means? The mutation has been transmitted to humans. I've got to tell Erica at The Cell; this changes the game entirely.

Dr. Motto and Dr. Lamont look at this while I call Erica."

Both doctors were flabbergasted at what they were looking at. How could this be possible? Where would a man contract the mutated super cell?

They needed to solve this new finding quickly as possible. Mankind may be in the midst of a worldwide pandemic about to happen.

"Excuse me Dr. Motto. What if this human is ground zero and he's the carrier, but immune to it's effects?" Jill asked.

"That's definitely a valid question and worthy of consideration. We need to examine this person ourselves and either rule him the cause or not." Dr. Motto said.

Dr. Zurich returned and told his two colleagues that he and Dr. Jones were going to Missoula to interview the man named Rodic.

Jill restated her theory of the human being ground zero for the mutations to Dr. Zurich.

He agreed that might be something to consider and would keep her hypothesis in mind.

KLAMATH FALLS, OREGON

Dr. Jones had given Dr. Botanic the run of her lab in her absence and had directed her staff to help him in any way he asked.

Captain Brown picked up Dr. Jones from The Cell's secret location and flew her to Atlanta. As they touched down in Atlanta, Dr Jones saw Doc on the tarmac.

Dr. Zurich was standing next to an F-15 that was being refueled.

Captain Brown and Dr. Jones exited their jet while the F-15's were both being refueled.

The two pilots and doctors met in the middle of the government secure staging area. They discussed the route and time to travel to Klamath Falls.

Once fueled the doctors put on their wraparound sunglasses and helmets, they knew the routine at this point. The two F-15's got clearance from the tower and each shot down the runway sixty seconds apart and disappeared into the clouds.

It was a beautiful sunny day and in the high seventies when the jets touched down in Klamath Falls. They hailed a cab and went straight to the police station.

Police Captain Roy Anders welcomed the visitors and explained that Rodic was being held at Bellevue Institute. He offered to escort them to the Institute and they graciously accepted.

It wasn't far outside the city limits to Bellevue Institute and they arrived in less than twenty minutes. Captain Anders introduced them to Ben Snow and explained who and why they were there.

"Pleasure to meet the both of you. I was given a heads-up that you were coming to evaluate the man called Rodic. This way please, but keep in mind he's becoming very irritable and has developed a short fuse when questioned."

"That's okay, we've been through a hell of a time already and he can't top that I'm sure," Dr. Zurich stated.

Mr. Snow led the two doctors to a cell that was really nicely furnished and had many necessities. When they reached where Rodic was being held, they found him staring at a large flat screen television.

They didn't know at that moment that he'd never seen one before.

"Excuse me Mr. Rodic. I'm Dr. Zurich and this is Dr. Jones. We'd like to talk to you and ask a few questions. Would that be okay with you sir?"

"I want to go back to my people; I know their worried about me. If talking with you will help me to returning back home, then it's okay."

The cell door was unlocked and the two doctors entered. The door remained opened; but two armed men stood guard on either side of the doorway.

"Thank you, I understand you go by the name of Rodic and nothing more than that. Is that the way you want to be addressed?"

"Yes."

"I've been advised of your statements already, so I won't ask you to repeat all of that again. Dr. Jones and I would like to know more about your bloodline and its origin. Do you know anything about how you came to have the blood you have?"

"I don't understand. I was born the way I am."

"You never heard stories about your ancestors or distant relatives?"

"Oh yes. The Goracks have kept our history for hundreds of years. We have murals on cave walls and on many lava tubes. They are all lost now and our legacy is gone and will be forgotten."

"No Rodic, part of why Dr. Jones and I came to see you was to find out about your peoples heritage. You can help us preserve the Goracks history for everyone to know forever."

"How can you do that when the evidence I spoke of is now buried in molten lava?"

"How many more Goracks are there living in the woods?"

"There was 200, but five stayed behind. There's only a hundred and ninety now. Five elders have died since our arrival on the surface."

"Would you please allow me and Dr. Jones to visit your people and talk to them like I have been with you?"

"Yes, the Goricks have nothing to hide. We want to see and understand the surface world. If I can leave, I will take you there."

"You can certainly leave. Dr. Jones and I work with the Government and we say you can leave."

"You can tell all these people to let me go and they have to obey what you say?"

"Yes Rodic, they have to do as I or Dr. Jones say."

"Let's go, I need to get back to my wife and children. I know they are worried about me"

"Captain Anders, could you take Rodic, Dr. Jones and I back to the Gorack's home?" Dr. Zurich asked.

"Sure, get in the squad car and I'll drive you up there. It's off the road somewhat and we'll have to walk about three-quarters of a mile to where Rodic lives." Captain Anders said.

Once out of town the road turned from asphalt into a dirt road and bumpy. They finally reached their destination; Captain Anders parked the car and they continued on foot to conclude their journey.

When they reached Rodic's people, his wife and children came running to met him. After hugs and kisses the Goracks gathered around inquiring as to what happened after he was taken away.

He explained his treatment and the wonders of the city. The Goracks awed at every detail Rodic explained. The biggest reaction was when he told them about the talking pictures coming from a flat box on the wall.

Rodic finally got around to introducing Doctors Jones and Zurich to the Goracks. He explained their reason for being there. The Goracks were excited that someone wanted to preserve their history and legacy.

The Goracks gathered around and Dr. Jones opened up the questioning.

"Can anyone tell me what they can remember about your history? It would be a tremendous help if someone could draw the pictures that were on the walls."

Several Goracks raised their hands and said they could draw the images and others said they could tell her their history.

"That's great! Why don't you three start drawing what you remember while you tell me your story. Here is some paper and pencils for you to use."

"My name is Follower Jong, but you can call me Jong," he said.

"Sorry Jong, I will use that name from now on. Please tell me your story. I'm going to record our conversation. Is that okay with you Jong?"

"What is record mean?" Jong questioned.

"I push this little button and then everything we say is saved inside so we can listen to it again later."

Jong and the other Goracks looked at each other and shrugged their shoulders. It was evident they didn't fully understand the concept, but no one disagreed.

"Our ancestor's go back hundreds if not thousands of years ago. The Goracks were once covered with hair from head to toe. As the decades passed our hair became thinner and thinner.

There were drawings depicting our evolving stages. With each new development we improved until you see us as we are presently. Along the process we became smarter and smarter. We developed tools for building things. Fire was not only for light; but for warmth, cooking meat and would frighten away rodents when we did not want them."

"How did you deal with death, health issues and bodily functions, Jong"

"We would relive ourselves in the river down stream from our home. We would bathe in the river above that area but still down river from our homes.

We tried to bury our dead, but it resulted in massive infestations of rats and other underground creatures. We began disposing of the dead by placing them in the water and the current would take them downstream. We believe that the river goes to the paradise land of souls."

"That's very interesting Jong. Your saying that your food supply was that of only rats and other underground varmints?"

"Yes, but the rats we lived on are slightly smaller in size than the animal (a deer) we're cooking over the fire."

"We here on the surface are having a problem with certain mammals and other species having the same blood as the Goracks. How do you think something like that could happen?"

"I don't know. We have never had interactions with anything from the surface world. Maybe they too have evolved over hundreds of years like the Goracks, since we have the same blood?"

While Dr. Jones was talking to Pang and some of the Gorack people, Dr. Zurich was getting blood samples. He also was collecting hair samples because it represents many traits of minerals, vitamins and much more important data.

The Goracks that had been drawing handed their renditions to Dr. Jones. She was amazed by the talent they had displayed on them.

"These are wonderful ladies. You did a great job; I didn't know you were so gifted."

It was a good thing that Rodic had been stuck with a needle already. The Goracks would have never agreed to such a procedure without him explaining to them he had done it and it was safe.

The doctors had accomplished what they came for. They were ready to return to their labs and start analyzing their new samples. They asked if the Goracks could stay where they were on BLM land and Captain Anders nodded affirmably.

Captain Anders told Rodic they could remain where they were if they stayed there and not move somewhere different. Rodic agreed that the Goracks would stay there.

The three reentered the squad car and went straight to the USAF Kingsley Field. Captain Brown was standing by two F-15's that had just been refueled.

"Were ready to depart doctors. Please get aboard, we've been ordered to report to the President in Washington D C." Captain Brown announced.

Dr. Zurich sat in the backseat of the cockpit and put on the required attire. Dr. Jones did the same in Captain Brown's F-15.

Captain Brown taxied out on the runway with the other jet trailing. He got the clearance he needed from the tower and the two jets shot down the runway 60 seconds apart.

WASHINGTON D C

President Black had talked to several doctors from the most prestige's collages in the world. He had considered their input referring to the issue at hand. They recommended doing autopsies on the dead mutated species that were washing up on beaches.

The President had summoned the following experts for a private meeting at the White House. Doctors Tylor, Jones, Lintner, Lamont, Mote, Motto, Brownstone, Stoner, Elvan and Vice President Morehouse.

These people collectively represented, The Cell, CDC, Institute of Oceanography and the Species Migration Patterns. These organizations were Project Discover's elite members.

After a day had passed, everyone arrived and assembled in the conference room in the White House. The President and Vice President entered the room. Everyone stood and clapped as they made their way to the podium.

"Thank you and please be seated. This is a friendly meeting. There's no press, cameras and I ordered all recording devices turned off in this room. We can't afford any leaks to the public. If there is a leak, I'll know it came from one of you and that won't be a good thing I can Promise.

So, stop walking on eggshells. You can disagree with me and tell me so if that's the way you truly feel about an issue or order.

The reason for calling this meeting with only you individuals is you're the brain power of Project Discover. I consulted with other experts from around the world. I've decided that I want an extensive autopsy done on each mutated species.

Let me be clear. When it comes to sharks, I'm not saying any old shark. I mean one of the huge mutated ones. That goes for the whales and octopus too.

Dr. Brownstone, you're the world's best authority on sharks. I want you to do the autopsies on a shark and an Orca whale.

Dr. Lintner, you're the expert in octopus and squid. I want you to preform an autopsy on a Box and Man of War jellyfish.

I know there are experts in genetics, DNA and cellular structures within this team. I want you people to work closely with the results gathered from those autopsies.

I want you to take to heart this piece of advice. When I say that I want an autopsy done on these creatures, I mean an in-depth and beyond a normal one.

Dr. Lintner, I want you to carefully study the three hearts that's in an octopus and each of the nine brains it has. Not just one brain; but each and every one, as well as each of the three hearts. I hope that's clear enough for you. Everyone, leave no stone overturned.

That goes for everyone involved with Project Discover. The world needs to know if this super cell is possible to cross over to humans.

I was informed before I came into the room that there are some humans that have the exact super cell flowing through their veins. However, they originated from an underground world according to their leader. That assumption is being investigated by Homeland Security and the FBI.

Remember, not a single word from this meeting is to be repeated outside this room. In conclusion, while you have been here, an extensive lab is being fitted in Honolulu, Hawaii.

The newest and most advanced equipment is being installed in a building I deemed public domain. It's on the waterfront so these huge specimens can easily be relocated inside the building.

Dr. Tylor, of the Institute of Oceanography, will be in charge of overseeing that they are preserved and safely transported from the water to inside the building.

I'm being told that a whale that has been getting towed from Alaska is a day away from arriving in Hawaii. I suggest we adjourn and you got to Hawaii. There is a transport aircraft sitting on the runway waiting for you to arrive.

Please have a nice flight. There's a bus outside waiting to take all of you to the airport. Thank you and may you discover all we need to eradicate this mutation."

"Mr. President, I have a live 55-foot shark in my procession in Hawaii. I was going to study it for any data it might reveal." Dr Tylor said.

"Put that on the back-burner Dr. Tylor. These autopsies are the highest priority I can assign to them." President Black sharply stated.

"Yes, Mr. President."

INSTITUTE OF OCEANOGRAPHY

It was a warm night as the C-17 transport plane descended and landed on the runway.

There was a bus standing by to take them to the newly equipped lab. They soon found that it was an abandon warehouse and the government had spray painted it inside and out.

As President Black had said, it was filled with the most recent high technological equipment that they would need to continue their research.

Each person had their own room with a full bathroom. There was a recreational room and a large kitchen with all the appliances possible.

Dr. Tylor received an email that the transported species would arrive by 8 AM the next morning. Everyone picked out their preferred room, took a shower and went to bed hoping for a good night's sleep.

Next morning the boat that was towing a 58-foot shark blew its horn and Dr. Tylor went out to oversee its delivery.

There was two heavy duty cranes and a large platform with wheels sitting on rail tracks.

Steel cables were wrapped around the shark. One cranes cable was attached on the shark's front cable and the other crane was attached to the back-end cable.

Dr. Tylor gave the signal and both cranes started lifting slowly in unison. Once the shark cleared the barge it had been strapped to, it was swung over to the platform on land.

Josh Hopper was the operator for the boat that towed the shark from Australia.

"Hey Doc, long time no see. How the hell you been?"

"Great Josh, nice to see you again. Did you have any problems bringing this massive piece of flesh?"

"Not really. I had one night where I had to maneuver around six-foot waves and wind gust. I managed and here I am.

There's a boat about seven-hours behind me bringing you a Box and Man-of-War Jellyfish. Wait until you see the size of the Man-of-War, you won't believe it Doc. I got to get back Doc. Thanks for everything, I'll see you later."

It was daylight and the first time Dr. Tylor could view the surroundings. He was surprised to see several armed guards patrolling the grounds.

He noticed the maintenance man holding a silver box and waving his arm to attract his attention.

Dr. Tylor walked up to him and asked, "What can I do for you?"

"Hello Doctor, I'm Bobby Smith and I'm the maintenance man. I wanted to know if you were ready to move the shark inside."

"Yes, that would be great Bobby."

Bobby pushed a button on the silver box and the large platform started moving forward.

"WOW! I didn't know that the platform was motorized. That'll make things a whole lot easier."

It took a little less than an hour for the shark to be completely inside the building and in its designated area for Dr. Brownstone and his team.

There were a dozen specially built cranes and heavy-duty steel structures to move the species inside the building. As the shark cleared the platform it was moved out from underneath the shark. When the platform was no longer an issue, the shark was lowered onto a special examining table.

Dr. Brownstone started opening the skull in order to study its brain. Other members of his team started on their assigned duties. Everyone had their orders. Each doctor was assigned a specific organ. So, the heart, lungs, kidneys and stomach each had a doctor all its own.

Time passed by rapidly and soon Dr. Tylor heard another horn blast. He went outside and was astonished to see a Man-of-War and a Box Jellyfish so large that they barley fit on the barge.

Dr. Tylor oversaw the unloading of the two creatures and their being brought inside the facility for autopsies.

A couple of hours later another horn blast brought Dr. Tylor outside. He was receiving a massive Orca whale that was lying on two barges that were hooked together.

Dr. Tylor recognized Captain Eric Tome who was operating the biggest tugboat he had ever seen.

They visited as the Orca was unloaded. It was all the two cranes could do to lift the enormous weight off the barges. It was slow for the rolling platform to carry the whale completely inside the facility. In fact, it was over six hours to complete the short distance.

There was a fear that the motor for pulling the platform was going to burn up and the whale would be stranded outside in the Hawaiian sun.

Nightfall was close at hand and the members on the autopsy teams were exhausted. Dr. Tylor know they were supposed to get results as fast as possible. He decided to put everyone on two 12-hour shifts.

Next morning, he met with the head of the autopsy teams and explained his idea. He allowed each of the three department heads to split their team up anyway they saw most fitting for results.

The three picked their day and night teams and assigned leadership to the individual that would be in charge on the night teams.

As the Project Discover team Doctors departed, Dr. Tylor's cell phone buzzed. It was David Cornell informing him that the shark they had in the secure area had died.

After all that work, planning and searching for a place to house such a large mammal, it turned out to be a waste of time.

Dr. Tylor, instructed David to draw several vials of blood and cut a dozen pieces of flesh from the carcass. He wanted the samples stored in a safe manner so he could perform research of his own at a later date.

That evening when the nightshift started relieving the dayshift there was a news cast that caught everyone's attention. Reports were coming in from all over the Pacific Rim and Alaska.

Hundreds of whales, jellyfish's and sharks were washing up on beaches dead. From South and North America, Australia, Philippines and several islands that are situated in the Pacific Ocean.

No one had seen a live enormous being from any species for more than two days. It was more important now than ever. If the mutation crossed over to the earth's population, would the people that have been infected going to die?

If that was the case, they had to find the cause and an antidote immediately. Hearing the news of the deaths Dr. Jones called Bill Wilson at the State Department.

"Bill, this is Dr. Jones. I know these autopsies are the Presidents number one priority. However, I heard the news about all the mutated species are dying or completely dead. If that's true, Dr. Motto is the worlds authority in genetics and prehistoric cellular development.

I think it would behoove us greatly if the President would allow Dr. Motto and I to return to Oregon and work with the Goracks. They are now the only living thing that have the super cell. They hold the answers to living with this mutated double helix. If there's an antidote, it's in their bodies bloodstream."

"I understand what you're saying and it's valid. I will propose it to the President and explain your reasoning to him. Stay close to the phone, I'll call you back with a decision in a few minutes."

Dr. Jones sat down and waited impatiently for the Presidents decision. It took less than ten- minutes for her phone to ring.

"Hello."

"I talked to the President and he's one-hundred percent onboard with you and Dr. Motto leaving and working with the Goracks. Pack up whatever you and Dr. Motto can carry in one carryon bag each. Captain Brown and Captain Snow will be there in four-hours to take you to Klamath Falls. Good luck Dr. Jones.

Oh! Dr. Jones, have Dr. Tylor call the President on the private line, he has the number. The President wants to tell him about you and Dr.

Mottos departure and he has some questions on the progress of the autopsies"

"Thank you, Bill."

Dr. Jones went and informed Dr. Motto that he was accompanying her to Oregon to work with the Goracks.

He was overjoyed by the news and went to his room and packed the bare necessities.

Jose Ramarao (Dr. Tylor's favorite taxi driver) picked the two Doctors up and swiftly delivered them to the once Kaneohe Bay Naval Base, now a Marine Base.

Captain Brown and Captain Snow were ready to go. Dr. Jones knew the routine, but first timer Dr. Motto had to be walked through the procedure in order to take off.

KLAMATH FALLS, OREGON

The two F-15's swopped out of the sky and touched down on the runway at Kingsley Field, one after the other.

Bill Wilson had called Captain Anders and explained who and why the doctors were arriving. The Captain was waiting as the jets taxied up to the proper staging area.

Dr. Jones and Motto climbed down and gave the pilots back their wraparound sunglasses and helmets.

"Welcome back Dr. Jones. I hope everything is good and you're not here because of an emergency."

"Nice to see you again Captain Anders. This is Dr. Motto and he's an authority on genetics and cellular structures. It's important for use to go back and work with the Goracks."

"I understand perfectly. The State Department called and explained the importance of your visit. Hop in the cruiser and I'll take you up to see Rodic and the Goracks.

By the way, I've got a couple of heavy-duty sleeping bags and two waterproof tents for you to use. I already gave Rodic several Coleman camp stoves and plenty propane canisters for them.

I had a dozen porta-potties delivered to them and they fell in love with them. It's funny in so many ways, but it's a good thing. I had three pick-up trucks of food delivered to them as well.

They threw up for a day or two. I was disgusted when I heard that their main diet was basically rats. Wait until you see their face's when they open a can of anything and start eating it.

It's sad in away, but satisfying in another. They love M n M peanuts and Hershey candy bars. I can't wait for you to see how far they have come in such a short amount of time."

The squad car finally made it to the Goracks homestead, for lack of another word to describe it. Rodic came running with open arms as did many of the women. They hugged Dr. Jones and shook Dr Motto's hand.

"It's wonderful to see you again Dr. Jones. In your absences the women have made many more drawings for you." Rodic said.

"That's great Rodic, I see that the Goracks are adapting to surface life quickly and liking it. This is Dr. Motto and he's going to help me with some more tests. Hopefully, he can find more extensive facts about your blood cells. He's an expert in that field."

Rodic led both doctors to the tents that Captain Alders had set up for them. Once they settled in, they got to work.

Dr. Motto took blood samples from two male adults and two female adults and one boy and girl teenager.

Dr. Jones sat with the women that had drawn more pictures for her to study. She was even more surprised by the pictures amazing detail. They were almost the quality of high-definition.

Dr. Jones and Motto spent four days with the Goracks. They did many environmental testing's far inside the lava tube for methane and radon gases, plus other air quality components.

One surprise that Dr. Motto wasn't looking for, was the heavy detection of sulfur dioxide over the designated safety range.

Dr. Jones took more blood, hair and skin samples. She even took fingernail clippings to analyze.

On the fourth and last day when Dr. Jones and Motto were packing up to leave, several of the Goracks began to cough and had runny noses. After being examined by Dr. Jones, it was determined that they had contracted the flu.

Rodic explained that Goracks never got sick until a day or two before their death. The symptoms that were displayed was nothing close to what they were seeing now.

"The Goracks have lived hundreds of years not being in contact with any of the viruses and bacteria of the surface world. I will have Captain Anders bring you some medications. He will explain when and how to administer it." Dr. Jones said.

Dr. Jones contacted Captain Anders on the radio he had left for the Goracks to get hold of him. Soon the police cruiser pulled up at the Goracks homestead and the doctors departed back to Klamath Falls.

Dr. Jones explained to Captain Anders the situation with the Goracks. She gave him a special phone number to call when he went to purchase the medication. She told him to have the pharmacist call that number and they would give him the authorization code for the government's payment division.

Captain Anders dropped the two doctors off at Kingsley Field. He realized the importance of delivering medication to the Goracks, so he left and went directly to the pharmacy.

Dr. Jones and Dr. Motto were early and had to wait for awhile for Captains Brown and Snow to arrive from Portland, Oregon's Ang Air Force Base.

Suddenly Dr. Motto pointed out to Dr. Jones two jest approaching from the north. It was indeed Captains Brown and Snow landing their F-15's on the runway. They climbed down and the four of them had lunch in the base cafeteria while the jets were being fueled.

Once refueling was completed, everyone boarded using the proper protocols and departed for Hawaii.

HAWAII

It wasn't long until both F-15's touched down safely in Hawaii. The State Department had one of its cars waiting for their arrival. Dr. Jones and Dr. Motto were swiftly taken to the research facility that they were working in before their departure.

The facility had been nick-named during their absence as, The Hope. Once back at the facility, both doctors retreated to their rooms for some much-needed sleep time.

The next morning when Dr. Jones and Dr. Motto were reunited with their teams, Dr. Tylor said he had an important message from Dr. Botanic who was still at The Cell facility.

Everyone gathered around and Dr. Tylor started to explain.

"Dr. Botanic knows the specialties of each one of you. He's requesting that each department do a cellular carbon dating procedure on each of the mutated species. He's interested in knowing when they contacted the beginning of their mutation.

Dr. Motto, would you oversee the testing, because you are an expert in the field of DNA, genetics and cellular construction."

"Yes, Dr. Tylor. I will see to that and work with anyone that has a question about the steps required to produce an accurate outcome."

One member from each team dedicated their time to the carbon dating of the cells found in their specimen. To the surprise of everyone, the results showed that only one year ago the mutation appeared in each specimen.

Dr. Jones and Dr. Motto decided to address the elephant in the room. How old is the Goracks cellular double helix?

They tested all six samples they had taken twice. They got the exact conclusion each time. The two men were 36 years old and the two women were 34 years old. The two children's test showed the young male's cells to be 12 years old and the female's cells to be 13 years old.

While they were with the Goracks, Dr. Jones had collected a few articles from several of the women. One thing that stuck in Dr. Jones's mind was a locket of hair that one of the women said she could have. She only asked it must be returned. It had been handed down through her family for many generations.

Dr. Jones went to her room and retrieved the locket. She carefully tested the cells that were present. Dr. Motto assisted to assure that the test was performed perfectly.

At the conclusion of the test, they just stared at one another.

"Run it again Erica," Dr. Motto said.

They ran the test again, only Dr. Motto was the lead this time. The results were the same. Dr. Motto signaled for Dr. Tylor to come over.

He joined them at their work station and Dr. Jones told him their results were astounding. They were able to carbon date the cells platelets from the hair, to be at least nine-hundred years old.

The result supported Rodic's story of the Goracks being a people going back hundreds of years. The pieces were beginning to slowly fall in place. The main questions however, were still unanswered and remained their focus.

The research teams at The Cell, CDC and The Hope were baffled to answer how a mutated cell from deep underground infected the surface.

As the teams continued to try and solve that question, some new data became available for their consideration. The results from the lava tube air being tested by the governments Department of Environmental Quality had been completed.

The results showed methane, nitrogen, argon, helium, neon, carbon monoxide and hydrogen. These gases are called, Volcanic Gasses. When one is exposed to them over long periods of time, they can cause several conditions to occur.

Another clue that was more than helpful. If the Goracks have been breathing these gases for hundreds of years. It was really a good chance they were altered cellularly slowly over time. They adjusted to their changes and became immune over the years of change to diseases that are associated with the dangers of inhaling them.

The teams had a possible bridge from the Gorack's super cells to the surface.

Dr. Tylor immediately called Don Masters, the world's leading volcanologist and geologist. He was working at the USGS California Volcano Observatory in Menlo Park, Ca.

Mr. Masters was excited to come to The Hope research facility and help out anyway he could. He was also thrilled to work with people he admired for years in their special fields. He had followed many of them by reading their papers and going to their seminars.

He caught the first plane out of LAX to Hawaii.

Jose was alerted to his arrival and was waiting for him as he landed.

Jose flagged him down by the description that Dr. Tylor had given him. He introduced himself and safely took Mr. Masters to The Hope facility where Dr. Tylor was outside waiting for him.

Dr. Tylor gave Jose a hundred-dollar bill and thanked him for picking up Mr. Masters on short notice. Jose gave him a thumbs up and a thank you and drove away.

"Welcome Mr. Masters, I hope your flight was satisfactory. I thank you for agreeing to come without hesitation. We can truly use your expertise in the volcano field to answer some questionable theories we have."

"I'm glad to come Dr. Tylor. I hope I can contribute something that advances your research. I'm a little intimidated by the big-name doctors working on this project. I've never worked with a Nobel Prize winner in the league of Austria's Dr. Botanic."

"Don't worry about that stuff. We're just one big family here and no one has an ego problem. We're all equal and mostly go by first names. The problem at hand is the issue we have to solve.

As far as Dr. Botanic goes. He's flying in from The Cell tomorrow. I'll introduce you to him. He comes off a little standish, but he's always in deep thought and doesn't want to be distracted, so don't take anything personal if he doesn't respond the way you'd like him to."

"Thank you for that information. Where would you like me to start Dr. Tylor?"

"Follow me and I'll show you your living quarters."

Dr. Tylor showed Mr. Masters his room, the cafeteria and introduced him to everyone that wasn't working because it wasn't their shift.

"I'll introduce the others to you at shift change. Right now, I'd like to go over what we suspect and how you can help. Follow me to my office so we can talk in private and I'll bring you up to speed."

"May I ask you Dr. Tylor why there are so many armed guards protecting this facility?"

"I think after our talk that all your questions will be answered and if not, I will try and answer anything you're still concerned about. Oh! By the way I need you to sign this non-disclosure agreement. Everyone working on Project Discover has to sign one."

As Mr. Masters was signing the agreement, Dr. Tylor explained that he would inform him on the different facilities names so he wouldn't be confused by them.

By the end of their conversation the shift change was underway. Dr. Tylor introduced Mr. Masters to the remaining team members.

Dr. Tylor interrupted the team after they came on duty.

"Attention, I have placed the air quality results from the Department of Environmental Quality on your work stations counter. I need team leaders once again to appoint one member to test those gases with the super cell for any similarities." Dr. Tylor said.

Mr. Masters holds many degrees, but he had always used Mr. instead of one of his degrees earned title. He felt that made him down to earth with co-workers and not someone flaunting his success.

"It's an honor to be working with all of you. I will be here to answer your questions on volcanos, lava and the properties found in lava and their steam," Mr. Masters said.

Next day Dr. Botanic arrived at The Hope facility. Jose took the doctors bag from the trunk and pointed him in the right direction to Dr. Tylor's office. The taxi left for the airport and another fare.

Dr. Botanic entered the large room and approached Dr. Tylor's office, when Dr. Tylor walked out his office door.

"Hey, Dr. Botanic. You should have called and I would have someone pick you up."

"Thank you, but I took a different flight and wasn't sure when I would arrive. I did manage to hail a cab and the driver said he was a good friend of yours. He said his name was Jose."

"Yes, Jose is my driver and good friend. He's who I would have sent to pick you up.

Come in the office and have a seat. Was there a particular reason you left The Cell?"

"Yes, Dr. Tylor. I have six young Komodo Dragons and I'm going to the Galapagos Islands and start their repopulation program."

"That's great news doctor. I'm sure the governments of Ecuador, Peru and Columbia will be very happy to hear that."

"Yes, they are. Bill Wilson talked to each one yesterday getting permission to fly over their air space and land at an airport. Captain Brown will meet me tomorrow at 9 AM at the Hawaiian airport and take me to Ecuador. Then I'll be helicoptered out to the Galapagos."

Later that day Dr. Tylor called an all team members staff meeting. Everyone gathered around to hear what was up.

"I need an update on the progress that each team has made. The President wants a direct conversation with me in an hour. I need results.

I could hear dissatisfaction in his voice ten minutes ago when he ordered me to furnish an update in an hour.

Dr. Brownstone, you're the head of the shark and whale team. What has your team uncovered?

"The brain, kidneys, lungs, gallbladder, stomach and other organs were perfect in every way. The only abnormality was the heart from both species. They both displayed an enormously enlarged heart. In fact, their hearts literally exploded.

As big as their hearts were, it couldn't supply blood fast enough as they rapidly grew in size. The hearts were the only organ to become bigger, the other organs stayed their regular size.

That fact alone would have caused death in less than a month in my expert opinion."

"Thank you, Dr. Brownstone, that is something highly irregular and definitely deserve being investigated further.

Dr. Lintner, what say you about your teams' findings on the jellyfish?"

"Dr. Tylor, I can repeat word by word what Dr. Brownstone said, except for shark and whale. My team had the exact results. All three hearts in the octopus were enlarged.

The Box and Portuguese Man of War hearts were also enlarged. All other organs in the two jellyfish and octopus were regular in size. Only their hearts were enlarged to the point that as Dr. Brownstone said, they exploded."

"Thank you, everyone has done a phenomenal job on Project Discover. I thank you for giving me data to sooth the President for now."

As promised the phone rang in exactly one hour from the Presidents earlier phone call.

"Hello Mr. President."

"What's the good news Dr Tylor? I didn't select you to head up this project to get no results. What has these elite minds come up with?" President Black asked.

"Mr. President, the reason that all the mutated species died is because their hearts exploded."

"What are you saying?"

"Mr. President, as each of the species grew larger and larger, their heart did as well. The problem was they grew bigger faster than their hearts did. They reached a point that the heart couldn't pump enough blood to their bodies so it exploded trying to do so."

"Does this mean I can discontinue this expensive Project Discover program? It's killing the country's budget."

"Mr. President, we aren't sure how the species were infected. We don't know if the Japanese nuclear meltdown provided a contributing factor. There was way too much radiation released into the Pacific Ocean. We need to confirm if it did or didn't play a part in the problem."

"Crap, you're right. We must find how this super cell was introduced to several species before its repeated down the line. Continue working Project Discover Dr. Tylor."

"Yes sir."

THE HOPE

"Dr. Jones, do you feel our team has gotten all the data from the Goracks that we can?" Dr. Tylor asked.

"I'm sure there is information that seems like nothing to them, but would be important to us."

"I was viewing the drawings that the Goracks draw for you. I think it would behoove us to try and visually see these images in their true environment."

"How in the world would we do that? According to Rodic, that area is at the bottom of a gigantic magma lake."

"He thinks that it is, but he doesn't know that to be exactly the truth. Have any of our team explored the lava tube Rodic said they followed to the surface?"

"Yes, Dr. Motto and I entered the tube and collected air samples. We didn't get very far down it before it got too hot for us."

"I've been pushing you pretty hard Erica. I'm going to send Dr. Zurich to Klamath Falls, because he's an authority in paleontology and Dr. Motto. He's familiar with the Gorack's and he's an expert in prehistoric genetics.

I don't know how we could have missed considering investigating the lava tube Rodic said they traveled to the surface in. We just took his word for it and that's definitely not scientific."

Dr. Jones was pleased she didn't have to go back and visit with the Goracks. Dr. Tylor was correct, she was worn out and needed some rest.

Dr. Tylor informed doctors Zurich and Motto as to the newly thought of inspecting the Goracks lava tube story. "If possible, push far down as you can. Lance, you've been inside the tube with Erica. She told me it got too hot for the both of you. How far down did you get?"

"Approximately 100 to 125 yards, but we were dressed in street clothes."

"That's an important issue along with the toxic air quality. I know where I can get water cooled fireproof suits and air filtered helmets so you can breathe a regulated oxygen blend.

How wide and tall is this lava tube Lance?"

"I measured it three times when Dr. Jones and I were doing the air quality tests. They were all the same, 12 feet wide and 16 feet high. It's one big lava tube doctor."

"If it's that big, why can't you ride 4 wheeled ATV's and take more testing equipment than you could carry on your person?"

"That sounds great Dr. Tylor, but how do we stop the high temperature from melting our equipment and having the ATV's fuel explode?" Dr. Motto stated.

"Okay Lance, lets shelve that idea for now. I'll call NASA and see if they have any ideas on how to overcome this hurdle. If it can be done, there're the boys to pull it off.

I'll let Captain Anders know your coming and arrange for your transportation to Oregon. Today's Tuesday, so Saturday morning is when you'll leave. I want time to hear back from NASA and a couple of others I need to call."

The three research facilities were working hard to find the effects of mixing gases with mutated cells. They needed to see a collation between the two entities that were present in the super cell.

Saturday finally came and all was in place. Captain Brown and Snow welcomed the two doctors when they walked out on the tarmac and climbed up to their seats in the F-15's.

In seconds they were pushed back into their seats as the jets shot down the runway.

They didn't know it yet, but Dr. Tylor had a surprise waiting for them when they arrive at the Gorack's homestead.

THE GORACKS

Captain Anders was waiting as the F-15's touched down at Kingsley Field. After their greetings and pleasantries, they got in the police cruiser and headed for the Goracks homestead.

When they arrived, they were taken back by several men in white lab coats scampering around the area.

Dr. Motto pointed out to Dr. Zurich two oddly modified ATV's and two suits that appeared to be spacesuits. Their appearance was the only thing they had in common with an astronaut's attire.

Both doctors approached the ATV's to get a closer look at their design and modifications.

They learned that the men responsible for the vehicles were experts from M I T and NASA.

The vehicles were constructed from highly flame and temperature resistant materials. They were coded with the tiles used on the space shuttle, but 10 times more resistant.

The fuel reservoirs were extremely experimental. They were made from a new compound material that had only been tested once on a small scale.

However, both NASA and M I T's mind trusts believed in its success, that it was approved for this mission. The tires were made of a secret material that no-one was allowed to talk about in any way. All they could say was that they wouldn't be an issue, unless they were to make contact with lava themselves.

The batteries were enclosed in the middle of the ATV's and shielded with the new material that was being used on the outside of the vehicles. The lights were an Argon and Neon gas mixtures to obtain a bright and resistant lamp.

That was exciting news for Dr. Motto and Zurich. They made their way over to the suits to see and hear about their functions and capabilities.

There were twice as many experts gathered around them than were at the ATV's. The suits were more important than the vehicles, so more attention was focused on them.

Experts from NASA, M I T, AAAS, NSF and from the RSS. These men and women represented the best minds in the world. They were from several countries and they assembled together on the request from President Black.

The experts weren't very forthcoming on details about the suit's modifications. The only real fact that they commented on, was that the suits had several layers of a liquid version of the tiles that covered the ATV's.

They weren't anymore helpful that that. Both Dr's. were somewhat concerned not knowing more about the suit's abilities.

Dr. Motto asked Dr. Zurich, "What about the temperature range or how the air supply is being controlled? What if the coolant isn't cool enough or stops working?"

"I have the same questions Dr. Motto. There are too many experimental issues being tested here. I feel we're guinea pigs and disposable. I'm going to call Dr. Tylor and bring him up to speed on our situation."

Dr. Zurich called Dr. Tylor and explained to him about Dr. Motto's and his concerns.

"Dr Zurich, I just got off the phone an hour ago with the President and was informed about the ATV's and suits that you will be using.

I was assured that they're safe as humanly possible. The President wouldn't have put his seal of approval on them if he thought you were in extortionary danger beyond the projected level, to abort the mission." Dr. Tylor told him.

"Thank you, Dr. Tylor, we needed to hear something positive. If the President has evaluated the facts and risks, it must be safe enough for us to continue."

Dr. Zurich and Dr. Motto had a good meal and turned in for the night. The next morning, they would start their journey deep inside the lava tube.

The new day came as the sun rose and its rays lit up the Goracks homestead.

The camp had breakfast and the two doctors proceeded to getting prepared for their assigned exploration. They got dressed in the bulky suits and received instructions on where important valves were located and their functions.

The most important was the air and coolant control dials. There were radio communication controls, but they weren't sure if they could be heard as they went deeper inside the tube.

The instructions for the ATV's was much simpler. They are easy to drive, turn and stop. They were shown the access to the fuel, battery and engine compartments. Each ATV had several go-cams attached to their roll bars.

The equipment that the doctors wanted to take with them was denied by the mind trust geniuses that had built everything. They did allow them to take an air quality, depth gauge and temperature devices. They had special specimen jars made at the NASA research lab.

They went to the opening of the lava tube and started the engines. They shook hands with Rodic, Captain Alders and gave a thumbs up as they entered the tube.

Everything was going smoothly as they slowly crept downward. It was only a four-degree angle that they were descending with. The lights lit the tube up like the strip in Las Vegas. All gauges were reading in the green and their suits were cool and air was sufficiently being pumped throughout the suit.

After an hour Dr. Motto called the experts on the surface for a radio check.

"Hello base, this is Project Discover calling home base. Can you hear me base?"

"Yes, Project Discover, we hear you loud and clear. We are also receiving a clear video from the go-cams. Everything is looking good. We're recording and monitoring every piece of data we're receiving."

"Great news, base. I'll check back in, in an hour, Project Discover out."

The two ATV's continued to push downward. The odometers for both showed 3.7 miles. They had been reset as they were about to enter the lava tube.

Dr. Zurich and Motto were amazed at how their journey was going. No problems to worry about or fix. They were cool and everything was still in the green. Nothing on their suits or ATV's showed signs of decay or melting.

They continued downward at a little faster pace because they were on mostly flat terrain at the moment. After an estimated quarter of a mile it was time to check in with base.

"Come in base, this is Project Discover," Dr Zurich said.

"We still hear you loud and clear and still have video connection. Hey Guys, this is a scrambled frequency. You don't have to use the project name and all that. You can say anything to get our attention. If you hear something on your radio, its us because no one else can piggyback this line."

"Okay guys, we can do that. We'll call you in an hour or so"

"NO! You'll call us back in an hour exactly. Do not vary from the protocols assigned to the mission, is that clear?"

"Yes sir, in an hour, out."

"Those Brainiac's think their God's gift to the planet. They need to be reminded who the hell we are." Dr. Motto said.

The ATV's continued downward and for the first time the temperature gauge needles lifted up slightly on both vehicles from the bottom of the green.

Everything else remained in the safe zone, but they would have to watch the temperature setting.

"Hey doc, you still hearing me?"

"Yes, it hasn't been an hour," said Dr. Motto.

"I know that. Did you notice a slight up-tick in your temperature?"

"Yes base, we made a note of it and are watching it closely for anymore rise. We'll keep you advised base, over and out."

Dr. Motto hung up and didn't give the surface crew time to respond.

"I thought these people were suppose to help us. It looks like they think we work for them and this is their mission," barked Dr. Motto.

"Your definitely right for sure. Lets just do what we're here for and we'll deal with them once we're back on the surface."

"Hey, what's that just ahead lying in the middle of the tube?" Dr Zurich said.

They drove up to the object and stopped. They got out of their ATV's and approached it.

"What the hell is that thing?" Dr. Motto asked.

"I don't know. I bet Rodic would know. I'll call base and see if they see this thing and if Rodic knows what the hell it is."

Dr. Zurich called the surface and asked them if they were able to see the strange object from one of the go-cams.

They couldn't, so they had Dr. Motto adjust one of the go-cams downward until the surface could see it in its entirety.

"Dr. Zurich, this Rodic. What you have there is what the Goracks have lived on for hundreds of years. It's what we have always referred to as a rat."

"A rat, it's the size of a Shetland Pony. You eat these creatures Rodic?"

"Yes, but when it's all you have, you develop a taste for them. That one looks like its only been dead for a day or two. It' surprising that other rats haven't eaten it already. If you really want to know how vicious they can be, open its mouth and view its teeth."

"I think it's more like a nutria, but it's a rodent as well. We'll continue to refer to them as rats., it's not that important." Dr. Zurich said.

Doctor Zurich kicked the body hard to make sure it was dead and not sleeping. It didn't move so he bent down and pried open its mouth. To his and Dr. Motto amazement the creature had six-inch K9's and the rest of the teeth were two inches long.

They were razor sharp and at a slight backward angle. Once it sank its teeth into something, they couldn't pull out of the rat's mouth.

"You're telling me you killed these creatures with just a pointed wooden spear?"

"Yes Dr. Zurich. If you come across a large golden spider. Run and do not try to get a better look at it. It's deadly and can jump ten-feet. It only attacks if you pressure it or it feels threatened. If you back away and leave it alone, it will do the same. Their rare, but they do live in the underground lava tubes."

"Do you want us to bring this rat back to the surface with us?" Dr. Zurich asked.

"No doctors, not under any circumstances are you to bring that thing back. It could have viruses, parasites or diseases we have never heard of before. Do you understand doctor?"

"Yes, I understand completely, over and out base."

They pulled the corpse off to the side and proceeded downward.

After a short time, they came across pictures drawn on the walls in the tube. Both doctors took pictures and made some notes for their report when they returned to the surface.

The story of the Goracks was illustrated from their beginnings to the present. The ladies that had drawn pictures for Dr. Jones had never seen these particular ones before. It was the first time any of them had been in this lava tube.

It showed in amazing detail how the Goracks once lived on the surface. Once the surface got so polluted and non-livable, they were forced to relocate underground.

The first Goracks that left the surface were pictured as what we would call prehistoric man. Each picture showed the process being made while adapting to their new world. The mural consisted of 24 stages of the Gorack's development.

Once documenting the drawings, they continued downward. Their temperature gauges had nudged upward a hair more. The heat was not an issue at the moment, but was concerning and warranted paying closer attention to.

After they had traveled one-hour, they came to a stop, so they could report back to base. As Dr. Motto was about to key up the mic, he noticed something strange fifty-yards ahead of them.

The two men exited the ATV's and approached the mysterious object slowly.

"Is that what I think those are?" asked Dr. Zurich.

"Yes, it's three skeletons that appear to be adults."

"Take some pictures of that necklace around that one's neck. I see the other two have bracelets on their wrist, take some pictures of them as well." Dr. Zurich said.

Dr. Motto called the surface, but the signal was weak and scratchy. The same was true of the response from the surface. After a few minutes and piecing together a word here and there, it was decided to return to the surface immediately.

Both men turned their ATV around and headed upward towards the surface. They hadn't said a word about the drawings or the skeletons they had discovered. They wanted to surprise the elites that they were more than capable to be entrusted with any highly sensitive missions.

THE HOPE

Dr. Tylor was receiving the data and the progress of his teams' efforts in Oregon. He was overjoyed that Dr's Zurich and Motto had descended so far down the lava tube. He was told that they were returning to the surface, but it would take four to five hours until they emerged from the mouth of the tube.

Dr. Tylor informed President Black of the underground mission. He also told him about three theories that the team was considering to solve the mutated super cell issue.

While the exploration of the lava tube in Oregon was transpiring, other ideas were being enacted. The Hope team wanted to rule out their 'maybes' and 'what if' theories. That was how they reached their final three theories, by disproving several other ones, leaving the three that were now being discussed.

THE DECEPTIVE

Captain bomber had the Deceptive headed for the Mariana Trench, the first place where the Deceptive had contact with the mutated shark.

The mission for the Deceptive was to investigated what was at the bottom of the trench. Did it have anything that could have played a part in the development of the huge sharks?

The Deceptive had the Challenger Deep onboard. It's an unmanned underwater vehicle that's capable of reaching the Mariana's depth of 35,768 feet. It's privately owned by Woods Hole Oceanographic Institute (WHOI).

The Institute loaned it to the government for this mission. The Institute sent its best operators to operate the vehicle and to answer any questions that might arise during testings. They probably wanted to make sure the vehicle wasn't lost or damaged. Dr. Rip Mote was from The Hope. He was there to take notes and make sure the correct samples were collected.

The Deceptive reached the area above the Mariana Trench. The remote-control vehicle was slowly lowered over the side and into the water. The operators did their regular diagnoses and made sure that the lights and cameras were functional and the batteries were fully charged.

Once it was clear that it was ready to dive, the vehicle disappeared beneath the surface.

Everyone gathered around the operator's laptop and watched the video that was streaming live coming from the vehicle. When the

Challenger Deep reached the bottom of the trench, the cameras began a sweep of the ocean floor.

To many of the onlookers it was a real eye opener. There was lava pouring out and creating huge mountains of cooled lava. They saw gallons of oil leaking into the ocean. There were countless steam vents spewing steam at a tremendous rate.

They saw many different species at that depth they would have never believed, if not for seeing them with their own eyes.

The vehicle took water samples from the steam vents and gathered some oil. It wasn't able to collect lava samples; but the vehicle circled above the lava as closely as it could and collected any gases being released.

The operators guided the vehicle back up to the surface. The Deceptive submerged just enough to allow the unmanned vehicle to hover over the submarine. Then the Deceptive rose up out of the water so that the vehicle could sit on the top of the sub.

Some of the crew went outside and locked the Challenger Deep down on the special holding bracket that had been installed just for its transportation.

The Deceptive returned to Hawaii. The drone's operators gave Dr. Mote the DVD of the vehicle's video. One of the operators went and gathered the samples that had been collected and gave them to Dr. Mote as well.

After handshaking and congratulations, the Challenger Deep was lifted and put on its own boat that had delivered it from Gaum. Dr. Mote hurriedly went to The Hope with the precious samples and the Deceptive went to it's slip there in Hawaii.

KLAMATH FALLS, OREGON

Dr's Zurich and Motto were totally exhausted as they exited the lava tube. They shielded their eyes from the bright sun and stepped off their ATV's.

"How was it guys? How far down did you actually get?" Captain Anders asked.

"I feel we achieved a lot. We gathered some data that I'm hoping will help Rodic in recalling more of the Goracks development." Dr. Motto said.

The elites were more interested in the ATV's than anything the doctors had to report. They were looking over every inch of the machines and writing down stuff by the pages. One guy was entering everything that was being said on his laptop.

"Did you see any Goracks on your journey?" Rodic asked.

"I don't know for sure Rodic. But I do have some pictures I want you to look at." Dr. Zurich said.

He showed Rodic the pictures and told him they came across three skeletons when they turned around to come home.

"I know who all three of these Goracks are. They're three of the five that stayed behind. Promise me that when you go back down the tube, you will bring their bone back with you. They deserve a proper burial and one is a follower's relative. I must go now and inform her the outcome of her cousin's decision to stay behind."

Rodic turned and slowly walked away sadly, knowing the affect it would have on his fellow Gorack's family. He wished he'd forced the five to come, but the truth was, it wasn't his place to force anyone to do as he says. But it still haunted him that he didn't.

THE GALAPAGOS ISLANDS

Dr. Botanic arrived at Puerto Villamil safely with his young Komodo Dragon's. He was met by Dr. Travor Little who had set up a research facility after the United States had eradicated the Komodo's nesting areas and any eggs that were discovered.

Dr. Little was monitoring the restoration of the destroyed foliage that had occurred. He was seeing that the habitat was returning properly and successfully growing on its own.

The humid climate was perfect for flourishing vegetation to thrive and be sustainable.

Dr. Botanic looked around and saw the landscape totally different than it had been some weeks before when he was there.

"Wow! Dr. Little. This is amazing results in reestablishing the environment back to its original state."

"Yes, it is Dr. Botanic. When you use the best seeds and nutrients this is the results you can count on. It also helps when money is no object and you can purchase anything that will help speed up the restoration."

"Well said doctor, there's nothing like a blank check from the United States Government to experiment personal theories and ideas on."

The two went to the research center that Dr. Little was living in and working out of. They went over the soil PH and other acids that were a concern. Dr. Little had been collecting that data for weeks from the three areas that Dr. Botanic had chosen for releasing the Komodo's.

Everything was perfect environmentally; even the creatures that Komodo's eat had retuned in fantastic amounts.

They got a good night's sleep and rose the next morning as the sun was rising over the Pacific. Dr. Botanic had picked the biggest, smallest and middle-sized islands for releasing the dragons.

Both men left the research center along with a local boat captain and a couple of men to carry and chop any heavy vegetation. It took most of the day to release two Komodo's on each of the three islands.

Dr. Little would stay there on the Galapagos Island and continue to monitor and report back to Dr. Tylor. The reason was that Dr. Tylor was the head of Project Discover and not Dr. Botanic.

Next day the transport helicopter picked Dr. Botanic up and returned him to Ecuador. However, the helicopter had to land at San Cristóbal for fuel coming and going. From Ecuador Captain Brown flew back to Hawaii. It was a long trip and Captain Brown had to refuel twice before finally touching down in Hawaii.

The reason for Dr. Little staying on the islands was to take blood samples from the dragons every two weeks to make sure the weren't evolving into the same mutated super cell. Each of the dragons had a miniature tracking device implanted under their skin so they could be located immediately.

It was an assumption that the Komodo's were the first to have shown the affects of their mutation. If that was the case, they would have been the first species to die off. That would prove that a land creature was the first ones infected.

That raised the question, why? What did the lizards, sharks and jellyfish have in common? Why were they the only three species that were acceptable to the super cell?

Between the CDC, The Cell and The Hope facilities, they had gathered millions of pieces of data. The answer was staring them in the face, but no one saw it so far. Then the Goracks part in the super cell. They were definitely the first to have the cell hundreds of years before now.

THE HOPE

Test results were coming in to The Hope facility from each of the other two facilities. A picture was developing, even though it was a slow one, it was becoming more focused.

The entire team at The Hope gathered around their conference table. They had taken many tests of Rodic's blood, skin, hair and even collected spinal fluid during his examinations.

Each doctor had his or her major issue that they needed to compare with their results from the different species they had evaluated.

Three similarities between Rodic's blood gases and the mutated species was highly important. Carbon Dioxide (CO_2), Oxygen (O_2) and PH, the amount of acid in the blood to see if there are any imbalances.

What allowed the heart to grow to an enormous size and the other organs stayed their normal size?

The testing and gathering samples were completed and all the results were in one place, The Hope facility.

That night was the beginning of many long days of brainstorming and dialogue about theories and comparisons. Each doctor explained their conclusions to the others and then defended them when there were questioned or met with pushback that denied the findings.

Everyone knew the process wasn't personal, but a way to confirm their findings as fact and not theory.

Dr. Botanic had arrived from the Galapagos Island and he too sat at the table. He listened mostly because he had only been a member of Project Discover for a short time. He had never been a member of a designated team, but he was weighing in on genetics and genealogical issues when he felt he could help.

THE GORACKS

While the Goracks were living in Oregon on BLM land, the Parks Department issued a memo that the water temperature in Crater Lake had risen by two degrees. That's worrisome for everyone, but a real matter to be concerned with when you know exactly what that represents.

Earthquakes were occurring all over the globe and major volcanos were erupting on every continent.

When that news was broadcasted over the major news outlets, Dr. Erica Jones left The Hope and returned to Oregon. She recalled something that Rodic had said that the Goracks controlled the earths pressure.

By doing that they could stop many eruptions and earthquakes.

She noticed right away that the sky was getting to be a grayish color from the smoke and ash.

Dr. Jones went through the ordeals of getting to the Goracks homestead. Captain Anders met her at Kingsley Field and drove her to the Goracks.

"Thank you, Captain Alders. I'll call you in a day or two when I need to leave."

"That will be fine Dr. Jones," Captain Anders said as pulled away and went back to Klamath Falls."

"Welcome back Dr. Jones," said Rodic.

"Hello Rodic. Can we go someplace where we can talk in private?"

"Sure Dr. Jones. Come this way."

The two walked a short distance into the woods. There were several large logs that were laying on the ground.

"Have a seat Dr. Jones. This is were I come when I want to be alone with my thoughts. Everyone knows not to bother me here unless it's an emergency. What has brought you here doctor? It must be very important and I'm betting it has to do with the changing sky."

"There's no fooling you Rodic. There's a problem with unexplainable earthquakes and volcanic eruptions. You once told me that the Goracks were the keepers of the surface world."

"Yes, that's true. For hundreds of years we have diverted the inner earths pressure so it didn't rise high enough to cause those kinds of catastrophes. Now that we're not there to monitor and divert the pressure, you are experiencing the earth's uncontrolled events."

"What can we do to correct the problem Rodic?"

"There's nothing anyone can do on the surface. The Goracks have wondered what would happen to earth if we ever stopped doing what we were. I guess we have seen the results from our absents. I am sorry it has become exactly what the Goracks have been saving the surface from."

"It's not your fault or the Goracks fault. The fact is you have protected the earth's surface for hundreds of years. I thank you and your ancestors for doing that.

I would like to get one more blood sample from you Rodic. I want to save it at the CDC and The Cell facilities."

"Anything to help you Dr. Jones, is doctors Motto and Zurich coming back to explore deeper into the lava tube?"

"I believe they are planning to return in a few days. I see the ATV's and Brainiac's from everywhere are still here. If it's okay with you, Id like to stay around for a day or two and talk with the women. I also need a day off to relieve my stress and anxiety."

"You're always welcome doctor. I'll see that my wife has fresh blankets for you and your tent has all you'll need for a short stay."

"Thank you Rodic."

The next two days were exactly what Dr. Jones needed. She hadn't even called The Hope to see if there had been any breakthrough. The fact they hadn't called her said they hadn't or they would have called her.

As Erica sat and was eating her eggs and drinking coffee, she asked Rodic to pass her the salt. As she reached out to take the shaker from his hand, she noticed how small the shaker looked.

"Rodic, has your hand always been that large or am I imagining that?"

'That's a strange thing that you noticed that. I was looking at my hands last night and I thought they looked bigger too."

"It's been a couple of months since you were weighed and I measured your height. I'll get my scale and tape. I have your medical data here on my laptop."

She brought up Rodic's medical statistics and displayed the primary general page. She weighed him and measured his height.

"Rodic, you're twenty-five pounds heavier and you're one full inch taller. I want to reexamine the four adults and two children I examined earlier."

"Yes, I'll get them for you. What do you think, that I'm different now than before?"

"I'm not sure Rodic. Hopefully I'll know more once I reexamine the others. Could you please go and send them to me Rodic? This is a very important discovery and could be a good thing or a devastating one."

As Rodic went to retrieve the six individuals Erica needed, she knew in her heart that it was slim to none that this development was a good one. She was ninety-nine percent it would be a bad omen for sure.

Rodic returned with the people Dr. Jones had evaluated before. She performed the same examination as she had before. The four adults had almost the same changes that Rodic had. They were a little heavier and an inch taller.

The two children had also gotten heavier and taller; but they were kids and that could be normal. Erica had to dismiss their new results based on that fact. She would never be able to distinguish between normal or mutated growth.

Erica called Captain Alder and informed him she was ready to leave. He said he would be there that afternoon and he would inform Captain Brown. He was still at Kingsley Field waiting to return Dr. Jones to Hawaii.

Later that day Captain Anders arrived and to Erica's surprise Dr. Motto and Dr. Zurich were exiting the patrol car.

"Small world Dr. Jones," shouted Dr. Motto.

The three of them swapped stories and updates concerning Project Discover. Doctor's Motto and Zurich were astonished by the revelation of the Goracks size differential.

Erica got in the cruiser with Captain Anders and they proceeded back to town. Dr Motto and Dr. Zurich were back to continue their exploration deep inside the lava tube.

They had a great venison dinner and kicked back with the NASA and MIT guys talking about theories and the sciences before turning in for the evening.

The next morning was a little chilly, but everyone was excited to get the exploring underway.

Rodic, interrupted the specialist and doctors as they prepared to start getting dressed and testing the equipment.

"Excuse me, I want to go down the lava tube. It's where my people come from and I know everything there is to know about the underworld. I should be allowed to be part of the journey."

"Rodic, you're not a scientist or have a doctrine in any field that would contribute to our research," said Dr. Zurich.

"You're trying to understand the underworld and what everything means. Why try to understand, when you have all the answers looking you in the face?"

"He makes a great point Dr. Zurich. He doesn't need a protective suit or air supply. The heat is no problem with him and he knows the way to his home area and section" said Dr. Motto.

"Are you sure you want to do this Rodic?"

"Yes Dr. Zurich, I'm ready right this second. Let's go."

The doctors started putting on their protective suits. The techs were explaining that they had modified the radio's and they should maintain surface contact at all times. They had also added more shielding to the fuel tanks for more protection.

They also altered the coolant supply to be cooler and a gallon more of it circulating.

It took an hour to get everything tested and checked out before the approval was given by all the techs.

Rodic road in the front ATV with Dr. Motto and Dr. Zurich followed close behind. With a hardy wave the two vehicles entered the lava tube.

The fact that they had already been several miles deep inside, they traveled at a much better speed. It only took two hours for them to reach the spot where they had turned around before.

Dr. Motto made the hour on the hour radio check in call. Every protocol was still in affect with no exception.

"How far would you say we are from where your home used to be Rodic?"

"Where halfway there, but it's under a lake of bubbling magma. I'm not sure how far up the lava came. We can keep going downward until we find the lava's level. Then I can tell you more accurately exactly where we are and answer any questions you have."

Dr. Motto nodded and slowly edged forward into the unexplored section of the tube.

"I want to thank you Dr. Motto for supporting me in my attempt to come with you. I miss my home Dr. Motto. I like all that the surface world has to offer and it's defiantly beautiful on the surface. But I love the underground world I was born and raised in. It's all I have ever known. Do you understand that Dr Motto?"

"I really do Rodic. We on the surface have a saying, there's no place like home."

"Did Dr. Jones tell you about my bigger hands and being taller? I'm worried about that. Do you think it's something I should be concerned about Dr. Motto?"

"I'm not going to lie to you Rodic, it doesn't sound like something good. That doesn't mean it's not, but honestly if it were me, I'd be worried too."

"If I get sick and about to die, will you bring me back down here? I don't want to die on the surface. Will you promise me that you'd do that Dr. Motto?'"

"Yes Rodic, I give you my word. If that ever happens, I will honor your wishes."

After an hour had passed, Dr. Zurich called the surface. Communications were still loud and clear. The heat gauge was still in the green and showed no signs of rising.

The ATV's continued downward before shortly coming to an end. They had the option of going to the left or right in the tube in front of them.

"Wow! I can't believe this isn't under lava. Turn left Dr. Motto. That's the way to my home. If this is above the lava's level, then maybe my home is too. I watched as the lava rose and swallowed all the Goracks homes, but it could have receded and our home is back as it was."

Dr. Motto turned left and traveled downward as Dr. Zurich followed. Dr. Motto slammed on the brakes and saw that he was 12 minutes over the hourly radio check. He called and as suspected the lecture was in high gear, after a five-minute venting, it stopped.

Dr. Motto simply said, "thank you," and turned the radio's volume down to zero.

They continued downward and Dr. Motto could see the excitement and joy in Rodic's face. Then in a split second the ATV's rolled out of the tube and into a huge cavern.

"STOP! Yelled Rodic. This is my home and the lava receded. Oh, wait until my people hear their home is still livable and not under magma."

"Hello base, hello base, Dr. Motto here."

"This is base, it's not been an hour yet."

"Listen you idiot. The Goracks homeland is intact. The lava has receded and this particular cavern is much cooler with a river running through it. Rodic is going to show us around and then we'll start back up to the surface. Don't worry, I'll call you when we start upwards."

He stopped communicating with the surface and Rodic explained how things worked in the cavern and his families personal home unit.

Dr. Zurich noticed that their air supply was just a little less than halve used and it would take the other half to return to the surface.

They turned the ATV's around and started upward and Dr. Zurich informed the surface they had started their return. They stopped so Rodic could collect the bones of the fallen Goracks. He changed his mind however, now that he knew his homeland was livable.

It took six hours for the ATF's to roll out of from the mouth of the lava tube and park on the surface.

Rodic dismounted in a hurry and ran to his families tent to tell them the good news.

After telling his family, Rodic rang the gathering bell. It was a signal that he had designated that would summon the entire homestead. Everyone stopped doing what they were involved in and gathered at the meeting area.

"I have good news to tell you. No! It's fantastic news to tell you. As you know I went with Dr. Motto back down into the lava tube. Our home is as we have known it for years. The magma has receded and our homes are as they were before the lava began rising.

We can go home and return to our true lives now," Rodic said.

There was a mumbling throughout the Gorack people. Their reaction to the news was unexpected to Rodic. He thought the Goracks would cheer and be jovial when they had heard the news.

He hadn't thought for a second, that the news would meet with any discontent or objection.

"I guess we should have meetings and discuss the options of returning or not to the underground," Rodic said.

The gathering broke up amongst whispers, crying and reservations. Rodic stood in silence and tried to evaluate his people's reactions. He couldn't clearly see any favoritism towards one side or the other. Their reactions were troublesome and one he couldn't explain.

THE HOPE

The results from the lava and steam vent samples collected at the deepest depths of the Mariana Trench had been completed. The air and gas samples taken in the lava tube, had also been evaluated.

All samples had been completed, the water and steam from Old Faithful in Yellowstone National Park. The gases from volcanos and the water from artesian wells.

Every DNA and cell tests were done and their conclusions were available. The oceans have 600 natural oil seep locations that allows one to five million barrels of oil to leak into them. Samples of oil from several of these oil seeps had also been evaluated and concluded.

The main focus was to find what genetic, cellular or DNA properties aligned with the Goracks super cell. There had to be a link for how the Goracks super cell came in contact with the four species on the surface world.

The team worked and studied as the weeks passed by. It was Dr Motto who had a special moment. He thought about something Rodic had said earlier. He it kept it to himself because it sounded like something so far out, he was afraid he would be ridiculed.

He asked Dr. Tylor if he would authorize him to return to Klamath Falls and speak to Rodic. When Dr. Tylor asked him what it was, he needed to ask Rodic, he said it was a theory and he needed to expand on a couple of facts.

Dr. Tylor gave his permission with the stipulation that he reports to him before anyone else. Dr. Motto agreed and started packing up some supplies.

Dr. Jones heard about Dr. Motto returning to see Rodic. She approached him and asked if he would do her a favor. He told her sure, anything you want Dr. Jones.

"Here are five medical charts. One is for Rodic and he will notify the other four upon your request. Would you please measure each one of these five people? I'm concerned about their weight, height and especially their hand size.

You can see in the charts that I have taken measurements from the tip of the thumb to the tip of the little finger while the hand is spread as far apart as possible. Please don't tell the others about these additions to their medical charts."

"I don't mind doing the procedure, but Dr. Tylor said I had to report to him before anyone else. I agreed with him Erica and I can't afford to lie to him."

"I understand completely. You honor your promise to him. I'll go and tell him what I asked you to do, that way you can reveal everything to him and not be burdened with a compromising decision."

Dr. Jones returned to the scientific discussion's going on in the conference room. They were doing better eliminating theories than narrowing down anything that could point to a super cell transference to other species.

Jose was outside as Dr. Motto exited the facility and got into the cab. In a few minutes the cab arrived at the Joint Base Pearl Harbor-Hickman.

Dr. Motto exited the cab with his one little carry on bag.

"Standard billing Jose. Bill Dr. Tylor and he will see that the government will pay you at the end of the month. Go ahead and give yourself a good tip when you submit the bill."

Captain Brown was ready to go as Dr. Motto approached the F-15 sitting on the tarmac.

"You're lucky Dr. Motto, I almost couldn't get our midair refueling, but I called in a couple of favors. We got to go now because we've got to be in the right place at the right time to refuel."

It was less than ten minuets before the F-15 went screaming down the runway.

KLAMATH FALLS

Dr. Motto was relieved as the wheels touched down at Kingsley Field and taxied up to the terminal. He climbed down from the rear seat and handed Captain Brown the helmet and wraparound glasses and thanked him for the ride.

Captain Anders was waiting for him as he entered the terminal.

"Hello Dr. Motto, long time no see," he said jokingly.

"How are you Captain?"

"Just peachy as always."

They got in the patrol car and were off to the mountain homestead of the Goracks.

They conversed during the ride by telling jokes, talking sports and a little politics to pass the time.

Rodic was surprised when Dr. Motto showed up unannounced. He was usually told in advanced when someone was going to arrive.

"Dr. Motto, what a surprise to see you again."

"Glad to see you again as well Rodic. I need to have a talk to you about something you said before about your underground world."

"Of course, Dr. Motto, anything you want to know or ask, I'll be glad to answer."

"First things first Rodic, Dr. Jones asked me to reexamine you and four others adults again and record your measurements today. She wants to compare any differences that might be present from your last exam."

"Sure, lets do it now. Follower Jong would you tell Bulia, Kirit and their wives to come to my tent?"

Dr. Motto did the five exams and he did see some discrepancies from their last exam, but that was for Dr. Jones to evaluate.

After a nice meal, Dr. Motto sat down with Rodic in his place of peacefulness in the woods.

"Thank you Rodic for allowing me to ask you more questions on short notice. You told me that once a year that the Goracks give a live sacrifice to the volcanos."

"Yes, we believed that by doing so, the lava would remain far below our homes."

"You also said that when Goracks died you put their bodies in the underground river."

"Yes, that is how the Goracks have dealt with the dead for generation after generation."

"You also said that the Goracks urinated and defecated in the underground river."

"Yes, that's true too. What's the reason you're asking this line of questioning? Why don't you just ask me what you're really searching for?"

"I've asked you the questions I needed to find the answers to the teams questions. You know me Rodic, we're friends, I wouldn't do anything to hurt or embarrass you.

Now that I have these answers, I can explain my theory to you and hear what you think about it."

"All right, explain your theory. I will listen and see if it has merit."

"Thank you Rodic. I think that after hundreds of years of putting the Gorack dead in the river and the Goracks bodily waste too, it caused an out of balance in the genetical and cellular structure of the established environmental norms.

I think that is how the mutation made its way to the surface. As the hundreds of years passed the mutation became more developed. I believe the muted cells were being released mainly through the steam vents and oil seeping.

The gases being released from the lava vents in the ocean contributed a small amount, I think, but can't prove at the moment.

I thought that since sharks don't develop cancer, they might hold a key to why they were acceptable to the super cell. That idea was put to rest when whales, jellyfish and Komodo Dragons contracted the mutation too.

Back in Hawaii they're trying to find simulations between all our samples and the super cell. They were getting close to arriving at a conclusive determination when I left.

What do you think about what I have said Rodic?"

"Dr. Jones told me that your team found the answer to why the infected species died off."

"Yes, they did and it was a monumental help to our research. I'm going back to Hawaii and present my theory to the team, thanks again Rodic. You've been an incredible help; we could have never got to this level of research without you."

Dr. Motto called Captain Anders and he was there in a short time and took him back to Kingsley Field.

Captain Brown called and set up the rendezvous point for the refueling. They left in a few minutes shielding their eyes because the sun was brighter than ever as they flew west.

Rodic had given the 190 Goracks two week for them to talk among themselves about whether to stay or return to their underground home.

Time was up and he rang the gathering bell loudly and longer than usually.

The Goracks assembled in the middle of the homestead and once they settled down Rodic addressed the congregation.

"I know that there has been a heavy burden on your shoulders for the last few weeks. This decision will be the biggest one that the Goracks will ever make. There's so much to consider pro or con.

I want to tell you my own beliefe on this opportunity. Everyone of you know that the earth is having massive earthquakes and violent volcanic eruptions on every continent. It was the Goracks that monitored the earths pressure and diverted it and stopped eruptions and earthquakes.

We have saved millions of lives and stopped devastation around the globe. It's the Goracks place and duty to maintain the honor and prestige of the Goracks legacy.

I was told that Follower Jong is representing a different position. You may speak Follower Jong and express your point of view."

"Thank you Rodic. Everyone here respects you and they hold no resentment towards you in anyway. We are at a point to agree to disagree. Here are some Goracks thoughts.

Since we exited the lava tube and have made a new homestead, it has grown on them. Organizations bring us many selections of food like we have never tasted before.

They're sick of eating rat's day after day. When Captain Anders arranged for the porta potties to be put in place and someone to come and clean them; that was satisfying beyond words for the women.

We have a large tent with a generator and a big screen to see images on. Captain calls it satellite television and electricity. We all like that, especially the children. They never laughed the way they do watching what's called cartoons.

Life is wonderful here Rodic. There's medicine when we get sick and doctors to keep us healthy. We have light and dark. Look at the sky and at night you can see stars that twinkle. We have been here for several months and have learned what things are and how to operated them.

The women love the square box called a microwave. They cook a meal in just minutes, not hours. Rodic, how can you not see why so many want to live on the surface?"

"I understand everything you said. I love all the same things you spoke of. I'm talking about our heritage. Isn't that more important than our comfort?"

"Do you know Rodic why our beneath the surface homestead is once again habitable?

The answer is an easy one Rodic. With the enormous increase in earthquakes and volcanic eruptions, the lava is being ejected on the surface.

If we return and go back to controlling the earths pressure, the magma will rise again and force us to the surface."

"Rodic, Rodic, may I offer another solution. I am Trerd."

"Yes, Trerd, say your peace."

"Thank you Rodic. Why can't we have both homesteads? We now have a pathway to and from both homesteads.

We have seen those machines (ATV's) go down the lava tube to our original homestead and return in one day to this one. If anyone gets sick, they come to the surface for medical help.

We don't have to eat rats anylonger, we can bring food down to those that choose the subterranean homestead. If the lava rises again, we can use the machines to return to the surface.

I think that solves every issue. The Goracks legacy and their duty to protect earth continues and we do it being comfortable. This is a blessing and we should not waste it by one way or another. My way everyone gets what they desire and there are no fighting or enemies made."

"That sounds like the perfect solution to me. I would give my vote to that offer if it were an option to vote on," said Rodic.

There was talking and buzzing amongst the congregation. It finally quieted down and Rodic again addressed the Gorack people.

"It's time to vote on the future of the Goracks. How many want to return to our underground homestead."

Roughly a third raised their hands along with Rodic's family.

"How many want to stay on the surface?"

The remaining Goracks raised their hand.

How many are in favor of the Goracks splitting into two homesteads?"

Everyone of the 190 Goracks raised their hands in approval.

"It's settled then, The Goracks will establish a two-homestead society. Would everyone that chose to return to our underground homestead come to my tent in an hour. We should address the when and time we will leave. We will need time to pack our belongings and say our goodbyes.

I will speak to Captain Anders about how to obtain several more of the ATV's. we need to travel as one unit the first time we return. I will tell him about our decision of two homesteads.

He will inform the correct people to our intensions. I hope they don't have issues with what we the Goracks, have decided." Rodic said.

Dr. Motto walked into The Hope facility to a smoldering atmosphere. It was clear that there was great tension hanging over the team as they were in heavy back and forth discussions.

Dr. Motto went straight to Dr. Tylor's office to give him his report first as promised.

"What's that all about Dr. Tylor?" He asked.

"You know Lance, the more I associate with great minds, the more their like children fighting over a toy in a sandbox. You must have seen this type of actions while working at the CDC?

I'm sick of trying to control their actions. I'm going to sit here and let them squabble amongst themselves until they finally see it's not the way to solve the issue at hand. I don't care if it takes all day, I'm not stepping in this time.

How was your trip to Oregon and did you find what you were hoping to find?"

"Yes Dr. Tylor, I believe I have a breakthrough theory that can explain most of our questions concerning the mutated super cell."

"That sounds excellent if it does indeed answer any of our questions. You can call me John if I can refer to you as Lance? The team and I must use the doctor word a few hundred times a day and I'm tired of hearing it."

"I agree with you John."

"Tell me your hypotheses on how the Goracks mutated cellular structure and their DNA became our problem on the surface."

Dr. Motto pulled out his notebook filled with notes that he had taken with his talks with Rodic.

John was truly impressed and thought it not only sounded feasible, but could possibly be exactly what had occurred. It was certainly the best solution that had been put forward thus far.

There was a quiet that embraced the facility and a mood of calmness. Both John and Lance opened Dr. Tylor office door and looked out over the facility's floor space.

Every one was working and no longer exchanging heated dialogue with each other.

"I told you Lance that they would come to their senses sooner or later. By the way Lance, our conversation and remarks are off the record, so don't repeat any part of them to anyone."

"You can count on me John, after all you didn't say anything that wasn't spot on."

"Thanks, you go and get some sleep and tomorrow morning as the day shift replaces the night shift. I want you to repeat your hypotheses to the team. I will appoint you as head of the research to prove or disprove your theory."

Dr. Motto went to his room and did exactly as he was ordered. He took a shower and went to bed and obtained his much-deserved sleep.

The next day Dr. Tylor held his total team meeting and gave Dr. Motto the floor to explain his theory. Upon completion of his presentation, Lance noticed that all most everyone of the team members had the look of acceptation in their eye and body movements.

As the team disassembled, Dr Jones came over to talk with Dr. Motto.

"Great theory Lance. I think it may hold many of our unanswered questions. I can't wait to see the research when completed.

Did you get the chance to examine the five subjects I asked you to do again?"

"Yes, I did Dr. Jones. I didn't enter their results into their medical charts because I'm not sure if I suppose to or not. Here is a thumb drive and all the results are on it. I will tell you the numbers have changed. I don't know if that's good or not, but I have a feeling you do."

Dr. Jones thank Lance and she retired to her room. It was her down time to sleep, but she quickly dove into the new results from her five Gorack patients' examinations. NO! NO! NO! she stated as she was entering the findings into their medical charts.

In just a few weeks Rodic had gained six more pounds and grew another inch taller. The same was true for the others that had been examined.

Why were the Goracks growing now that they were on the surface? What was the connection between the four earthly species and the

Goracks? There had to be a symbiotic element that was causing the cross contamination between them.

Dr. Tylor halted the round the clock research teams and went back to only one 12-hour shift. He felt that all their minds were needed to work together now that they only had one issue to focus on.

Dr. Motto was the expert in the fields of genetics and genealogy. He approached the task differently from the others. He started by trying experiments with what could affect the alteration of a cell's development.

The Ultraviolet Rays (radiation) in the sunlight has many different affects on cells such as the human epidermal pigment melanin turning cancerous.

Gamma Rays also come from the sun's rays every time there's a solar flare (radiation) adding more hazards for earth. They represent the most dangerous radiation.

Dr. Motto believed that the meltdown of the Japanese Fukushima Daiichi Nuclear Power Plant, March11, 2011, added more radioactive material to the existent levels of exposures.

There's over a dozen or more parts that make up a cells structure. Dr Motto had to test his theory with each one of those parts individually. It was a long and tedious operation before coming to a final conclusion.

Dr. Jones meantime was relentlessly slaving away with her delima of solving the cause of Rodic's apparent growth. Even though she wasn't as well conversed as Dr. Motto was in genetics, she was still a formable coworker in that field as well.

She managed to get a response when she introduced Ultra Violet rays with the mutated super cells lipids. The cells shape immediately changed before her eyes. She continued to watch and record the event for three hours.

The new creation she developed after an hour began to grow. She had put the view of the super cell on the large plasma screen for anyone to watch. As she viewed the image it exploded without any noticeable warning.

Had she found the causes and answer to why the four species had grown so large? Was that what Rodic was experiencing? She went straight to Dr. Motto, the genetic expert.

She explained what she had done and what the results were. He had been so involved with his own project, that he wasn't aware of Erica's testing or plasma display.

"Fantastic!" Dr. Motto said. "Erica, you might have found the master key that will open every door to solve Project Liberty. Do we still have some viable Rodic blood samples here?"

"I'm sure we do Lance. I'll go and see if we do, how much do you need?"

"One CC will be enough for now."

Erica left and returned in a few minutes with the required amount of blood Dr. Motto had requested.

He repeated the procedure's that Dr. Jones had performed, but on a larger scale than hers. He placed several of the cells that he had bombarded with radiation under the electron microscope. He redirected the image onto the plasma screen that was void of anything since the previous image had exploded.

He and Erica put two TV dinners in the microwave. When the bell went off, they removed their meals and went to the breakroom table in front of the plasma. They sat, ate and took notes virtually every other minute as they watched what was developing on the screen.

Time passed, but as before with Erica's test, the eight cells that Lance was testing exploded as well.

Even though the both of them were ecstatic, that still wasn't enough to announce they had the answers. They retrieved several mutated cells from each of the four species and put each of them through the same procedure as Rodic's were.

Dr. Tylor summoned Drs. Motto and Jones to his office. He wanted to know what they were involved in. He had noticed them and by their body language knew they were in deep thought about something.

They showed him the results of the many tests on their iPod's. They had uploaded videos periodically of the cells journey from start to it exploding.

Dr. Tylor was amazed by not only what he was seeing, but what it represented to help Project Discover come to a close and finalize the mystery.

"Right now, you're running the same tests on the four species cells to see if you get the same results?" Dr. Tylor asked.

"Yes John. We're just waiting for the results. That should be coming in about two hours from now," Erica said.

"As soon as those results come known to you, tell me first, no matter the outcome. Then I want you to go back to Oregon and see to the safety of Rodic and the Goracks." Dr. Tylor said

"We both agree a hundred percent with you John about the Goracks safety. The Goracks have become our family and friends for life." Dr. Motto said.

Dr. Tylor called Thomas Elvan (head of Species Migration Patterns) and Ben Wilson (State Department) via a three-way conference call. He explained where Project Discover was at the present time. He was careful not to say something that would represent they had solved the questions being asked of them. He did say they were making great strides forward and were hopeful they would lead them closer to solving the issue.

"I'll inform the President of your progress and let him know of your implication of success." Ben said.

Dr. Tylor began to think that on second thought, he should have toned down his remarks. What was done was done, so he decided to get on with the team's research.

It was less than ten-minutes when his government secured line phone rang. He picked up the receiver and said "Hello, this is Dr. Tylor."

"Good afternoon Dr. Tylor. This is President Black. I hear Project Discover is doing well and that you're close to solving these super cell troubles, is that true doctor?"

"We are getting close to figuring out how this thing started Mr. President. There are hundreds of moving parts that accumulated into one deadly mutated cell and caused this perfect storm."

"Sounds great Dr. Tylor. I'm going on a trip soon; you have Bill's cell number. If you need me for any reason, call him. He knows how to contact me under any situation. Have a nice day Dr. Tylor."

The president hung up as he was saying the last syllable of Tylor. John didn't even have the chance to say good-bye to him.

Shortly, Dr. Jones and Motto returned and informed Dr. Tylor that every test they had ran, coincided with each of the others perfectly.

"I felt they would. It's gotten late, so why don't you get a good night's sleep and leave in the morning? I'll call Bill and have him set up departure time and refueling with Captain Brown," Dr. Tylor said.

"That sounds good to us John. Could we have departing around ten AM instead of the six or seven Am time. We're both exhausted, Erica pulled virtually a double shift."

"Your right Lance, she did indeed. I'll make sure I arrange it for ten AM."

They went back to their rooms and John called and made the necessary arrangements for the trip to Oregon.

Next morning there was plenty of time for Lance and Erica to have a hot breakfast and make it to the airfield by ten.

Soon they were flying high above the clouds as Captain Brown and Captain Snow banked their aircrafts hard left and headed east.

KLAMATH FALLS, OREGON

As both F-15's touched down at Kingsley Field the police cruiser arrived. As the doctors climbed down from the jets and had handed over their flight gear, they were met by a stranger.

"Hello folks, I'm Deputy Allen Looms. Captain Anders is on a special assignment and asked me to escort you to see Rodic," he said.

"Glad to meet you Deputy. I'm Dr. Motto and this is Dr. Jones. I'm glad your Captain made arrangements for our transportation."

They entered the patrol car and Deputy Looms drove them to the Goracks homestead. They were shocked as they approached the Goracks home.

There were several black Secret Service vehicles and Captain Anders standing next to his patrol car. There were a least ten men with assault weapons slung around their head and shoulders guarding the area.

As Dr. Motto walked over to see what had drawn so much attention, he was surprised to see President Black having a conversation with Rodic.

Bill Wilson was standing next to the President carefully directing his security teams' moments.

"I see Dr. Motto and Jones have arrived. Join us if you would please. I must admit I am at a loss with most of the terminology interpretation I'm receiving from Bill. He tries though, but I need to understand the precise predicament we are in." President Black explained.

"Yes, Mister President. What are you needing to know first?" Dr. Motto asked.

"Did you or did you not come to an affinitive answer to how the mutation was started and how did it affect our species?"

"Our best theory is that the Goracks have been polluting the water and to a smaller degree, the magma underground for centuries. With the hundreds of steam and lava vents spread all over the ocean floor, small particles were released into our waters.

I'll use the shark as an example, but it represents the same evolution as the other species. The contamination started probably a millennium ago, with every year of breeding the more the mutation was advanced. Even though it would be little, it was that fact of little by little that no one saw or discovered it mutating the hosts cells.

That same evolution is what happened to the Goracks as well. Their cells are more advanced than the sharks are right now. The Project Discover team didn't find the answer to killing the mutated cells, it was nature herself that came to the rescue.

Dr. Jones and I recently working on Dr. Jones's hypotheses of why the sharks died, basically at the same time within one day.

The Ultraviolet Rays and Gamma Rays that are released from the sun and solar flares consist of radiation. When the Japanese nuclear plant melted down, it polluted the Pacific with enormous amounts of radioactive water and contaminants. The addition of that amount of highly graded radiation was enough to speed up the advancement of the already existent super cells.

The basic body was growing faster than the hosts heart. The heart tried to keep up the blood flow needed for the body, but it couldn't. The heart exploded due to working harder than it was designed to do.

I'm worried about the Goracks reaction to the sun's rays. There growing like the sharks did, but at a much slower pace. I need to discuss options with Rodic about the future of the Goracks. Have I explained efficiently enough Mister President or do you have any questions?"

"I have many questions, but not all of them concern cellular and DNA science stuff. I also need to know if there's a chance the American people could be infected with this Mutated cell? Is the next breeding cycle going to spawn another group of super cell species? Where are we on issues like those kinds of future problems?"

"Great questions and ones that definitely need answering Mister President. I have my team at The Cell working to solve those kinds of issues. I can say without hesitation that there is no chance of the population acquiring the super cell, furthermore the completion of the mutated level now present.

As far as the next generation of sharks having the mutated cells is a possibility. That's one of the assignments I gave directly to Dr. Mote two weeks ago. So, Mister President, that concern is already being explored.

I know that Dr. Zurich from the CDC has his team working on discovering a virus or bacterial agent to kill the mutated cells and not harm anything else. It's the same premise as that weed killer that just kills the weeds and is safe for you and your pets. It only kills weeds and not your grass. I'm sorry to equate the problem to such an example, but that's what it truly amounts too." Dr. Jones explained.

"I can see I have the right people working on Project Discover. Thanks to the both of you for your expertise in this matter.

I would like to see this lava tube that the Gorack people used to escaped to the surface." President Black said.

The security teams, the doctors and Rodic made their way to the entrance of the lava tube.

"So, Rodic. This is the tube that a hundred and ninety-five people used to reach the surface?"

"It was our only way to escape the rising magma Mr. President. What's amazing is that Follower Jong discovered this lava tube eleven days before we determined we had to leave.

It took weeks and if it would have taken a day or two more, many would have died. We ran out of food and water. We found out after my ATV trip back to my home, that it's 22 miles from here to there.

We haven't estimated how far below the surface we were yet. It's something we will address later when things settle down to a less hectic atmosphere."

"I'm glad your people made it. God must have been looking over you all for sure."

"Who."

"Never mind right now Rodic. As you said after it calms down, I'm sure you'll have it explained to you."

"Thank you, Mr. President"

"Alright fellas, get me back to Kingsley Field and get the wheels up. I've got a dinner engagement at the White House, move it guys. I've got a long way to go and a short time to get there' as Jerry Reed said in one of his great songs."

The President and his Secret Service team departed along with both police vehicles. Dr. Jones motioned to Rodic to come over to her, as he was waving to the departing cars.

He approached and shook her hand with a huge smile on his face.

"Your President is a good man. I enjoyed his visit. I hope I can meet him again in the near future."

"I need to have a serious talk with you about the Goracks future."

"We have settled that between ourselves Dr. Jones."

"I heard about that from Dr. Motto. However, things have changed to such a degree that may no longer be an option for the Goracks"

"That doesn't affect me, because I want to return to my original home. There are many that want to stay. They are the ones that will be disappointed."

"If you will ring the assembling bell this evening, Dr. Motto will explain to everyone what's happened. He's the expert in genetics and genealogy. He can answer questions that the Goracks will surly ask better than I can."

"Okay Dr. Jones, I'll call for the meeting after dinner. I just hope the ones that want to stay won't become violent. Goracks are slow to anger, but once they reach that point it can become vicious."

"Thanks for the heads up Rodic, but that won't change what has happened or reverse what's taken place."

"Let's drop the matter and see what happens at the meeting tonight. It's time to eat dinner Dr. Jones. Will you go and find Dr. Motto and come to my tent and share a meal with my family."

"Yes, I see him over there talking to Follower Jong. I'll get him and we'll be right there in a minute or two."

She went over to Lance and explained what Rodic had described to her about the reaction he might get when telling the news about their future.

"It has to be done Erica; they deserve to know the consequences if they stay on the surface."

"Rodic invited us to have dinner with him and his family. I told him we would be honored. He's waiting on us now, so we better go join him."

After a good meal and friendly conservation, it was time to face the music and tell the Gorack people the facts about their future.

Rodic rang the assembling bell several time and the people gathered in the center of their homestead.

"Thank you for coming fellow Goracks. Dr. Motto has an important message to talk to you about. I ask that you not hold the good doctor at fault for what he's about to tell you. Dr. Motto, the gathering is yours." Rodic said.

"Good evening everyone. I unfortunately have some disturbing news that I must pass along to you tonight. It brings me no pleasure to inform you of this matter, but you have the right to know.

I am aware that you have noticed a growth spurt with yourself and other Goracks. There's a reason for that to be occurring. It has to do with your body cells, DNA and reaction to certain things that you have never been exposed to before.

Since your cellular DNA and your double helix being so far developed, it is absorbing the suns dangerous rays. Your metabolism is reacting at a much faster speed than the super cell had on our species for that exact reason.

The Goracks are mimicking what our surface species did. They got bigger and their hearts couldn't pump enough blood to satisfy the body. Their hearts exploded and if you stay on the surface you will suffer the same outcome."

A loud mumbling spread throughout the collection of Goracks, followed by shouting and jeering.

"Why should we believe you? How do you know that's what's going to happen? I think you're a liar and a fraud," screamed someone from the crowd.

"Why would I lie to you. I'm trying to save your life's and warn you about what's going to happen if you don't take appropriate action."

"Go home and leave us alone, we don't need you anymore, just go away," again someone from the crowd.

"Calm down everyone, it's not Dr. Mottos fault. Didn't he tell you the truth about you growing taller and putting on weight? You have to know that being exposed to the sunlight is something our flesh has never been exposed to before. You mean you can't even think for a second, that it could have an affect on our bodies one way or another?" Rodic stated.

The gathering went silent as Rodic spoke. They could tell by his tone and demeaner that he was embarrassed because of their reaction to hearing what they were told. He understood their disappointment, but not the insulting of Dr. Motto.

The Goracks broke up and returned to their tents to discussed the news they had just received.

It was late and dark, but Dr. Motto and Erica didn't feel safe any longer staying the night. Lance called Captain Anders and he soon appeared in his squad car.

Hello doctors, what happened that you want to leave? You have always stayed the night as far as I can remember?" Captain Anders asked.

"We had to reveal some facts about the future of the Goracks and let's just say it wasn't well received. Dr Motto said.

"You mean you honestly thought that someone might hurt you?"

"Yes, we did Captain. Rodic told us what the Goracks were capably of when hearing bad news. In fact, he also thought it would be better if we left."

"Are you going to Kingsley Field?"

"No, we're going to stay at a hotel in the city. Where would you recommend for us to stay Captain?"

"I'd say Shilo Inn Suites, it's really nice and not far from Kingsley Field."

"Thanks Captain, would you please take us there?"

Captain Anders dropped the two off in front of the Inns entrance and they proceeded to check in. They got separate rooms across from one another to stay close incase something should happen.

Lance called Bill Wilson and asked him to arrange for their transportation back to Hawaii. It turned out both captains Brown and Snow were at Kingsley Field already. The F-15's had just completed their scheduled maintenance and were cleared to fly.

HAWAII, THE HOPE

At great expense, the government flew the remaining research staffs from The Cell and CDC to Hawaii. The Hope had the most advanced equipment and was large enough to house everyone.

It was time for a massive collaboration between forty of the most brilliant minds working on Project Discover. Bill Wilson believed that this was the fastest way get the answers the President wanted.

After two days had passed of bringing everyone to Hawaii, the sea of white lab coats was sitting in the huge conference room.

Dr. Tylor stood and to explain their task.

"I would like for you to work among yourselves for today. The next day will be a question and answer day, where your colleagues can ask for more detailed information on anyone's remarks. Day three's agenda will depend on the outcome of day two's results."

The original staff members of each of the two facilities joined back together for discussions. Doctors that weren't with either facilities (like Dr. Botanic) were rovers and dropped in on the conversations where ever they chose.

WASHINGTON D C

The meeting that President Black had when he left Oregon was more than just a dinner. It was a dinner that got public announcements or press coverage.

It was a summit meeting with the heads of several countries to discuss options about the globe's environmental issues. There were volcanic eruptions happening somewhere on earth every day.

Earthquakes by the dozens were occurring day after day. Each week they grew higher on the Richter scale. What had started in the five-point three range, was now in the seven-point two range.

If a solution wasn't found in the next two or three weeks to subdue them, the damage and the deaths of millions would be devastating.

The sun was close to being an object behind a curtain. The more ash and smoke that was being released was causing the sky to grow darker, a little at a time.

This wasn't just the United States of America's problem, it was everyone's problem. No country was spared, they all suffered the same plight as the U S.

The answer to why this was happening had already been explained. In fact, right down to the exact time and why. Like most government bureaucrats, no one was listening.

The world leaders for the first time in many years didn't gang up and blame the United States. That was because the earthquakes and eruptions was happening in their countries as well as America. Everyone was responsible as far as the political leaders were concerned.

They went late into the night trying to figure out what if anything they could do. Not one individual had a solution, including President Black. What a moment in history, politicians getting assembled and no one could blame someone or have a word to say.

KLAMATH FALLS, OREGON

The Goracks were still at odds upon hearing and accepting what Dr. Motto had revealed to them. Some cried and others dealt with the revelation by laughing to mask their feelings. A few sat quietly and stared out at the trees as if in a heavy depressive state.

Rodic called Captain Anders and asked him to contact Dr. Jones and see if she would send someone from the government to talk to him.

The Captain agreed naturally and made a call to Dr. Jones. He relayed Rodic's message to her and she then called Bill Wilson with the request.

Within 24 hours Bill Wilson was standing in front of Rodic's tent. Rodic came out and met with him. Rodic remembered seeing Mr. Wilson when he was visiting with President Black at their homestead.

"Thank you for coming sir. I remember you from the last time you were here. I'm sorry, but I don't recall your name."

"I'm Bill Wilson and I'm with the State Department of the United States. I have the authority to negotiate with you and the Gorack people.

You requested someone from the government to come and have a talk with you. I'm here via your wishes, what would you like to say?"

"Dr. Motto made it clear, that if the Goracks stay aboveground, we will die. As leader of my people, I want another opinion from someone not involved with your research team. I want an outsider to evaluate the facts and come to their conclusions."

"I understand your hesitation about what Dr. Motto said. I will see that your request is assigned to a world-renowned scientist. I will let President Black know of our talking points and he will choose the person to re-evaluate the data. Is that acceptable to you Rodic?"

"Yes, if the President himself appoints someone he feels is honest and fair, I will accept the outcome."

"Good, I'll leave now and set this in motion. It may only take three or four days to have your answer. All the facts have already been determined. The only thing left is for a scientist to either verify or not the facts as they are now determined."

Bill departed along with his four-man security team that was always by his side. They soon arrived at Kingsley Field where Air Force 2 was fueled and ready to return to Washington D C.

WASHINGTON D C

Bill called the President once he was airborne and had access to the secured government phoneline. He explained to President Black what Rodic had requested and that he approved of the action.

The President also agreed and told Mr. Wilson that by the time of his return, he would have a name and consent of someone worthy.

As Air Force 2 touched down on the runway at Dulles, Captains Brown and Snow that had flown their F-15's for protection, followed behind the 757.

The two captains were getting proficient in midair refueling of the F-15's. It's not very often that occurs over the United States for safety reasons. However, this was a special circumstance because flying could come to a halt if more smoke and ash darkened the skies.

Mr. Wilson went straight to the White House and was immediately sent to the Oval Office. He knocked and heard the Presidents voice, "Come in."

"Thank you, Mister President."

"How was your flight Bill?"

"A little bumpy over the Rockies, but other than that, perfect."

"I talked to Professor Kovicha in Romania. He's on a flight as we speak to New York. He's going to be met by a couple of FBI agents. They will fly with him to Hawaii and deliver him to The Hope facility. He is well known in the scientific world and every think tank organization there is."

"That sounds great Mister President. Sounds like you have taken care of every step from start to finish."

"I think so Bill. Why don't you go home, see the family and get some sleep? I know how those long flights can get you down. Oh! I also called Dr. Tylor and gave him a head's up on Professor Kovicha's arrival."

"May I ask how your meeting went with the other heads of states?"

"Lets me put it this way. We had pleasant conversations, told some jokes and made plans for future visitations. We otherwise made no progress on the environmental issues. We couldn't even come up with one single idea or theory. We were total failures in that department."

"I'm sorry to hear that sir. I guess it comes down to Dr. Tylor's Project Discover team to save the world as we know it."

Professor Kovicha's plane landed at JFK airport and the passengers were ordered to the custom authority's entry station.

The two FBI men walked up and flashed their badges to the custom officials and introduced themselves to the professor. One of the agents picked up the professor's bag and the three left. The professor didn't have to go through customs, he was considered a government guest of President Black.

They went to the governmental security section where a Marine White Hawk helicopter was waiting. It's only 240 miles from JFK to Dulles and the white hawk has a 350-mile range.

The boarded the chopper and headed to Dulles. Air Force two was being fueled and cleaned at Dulles for its turnaround flight to take Professor Kovicha to Hawaii.

Vice President Richard Morehouse met the Professor when he exited the White Hawk at Dulles. He thanked the Professor for helping in this important matter and made apologies for President Black not being able to meet him personally, due to unexpected emergencies.

The professor and four Secret Service men entered Air Force two. The two pilots and two stewardesses were already onboard. In a matter of minutes, the plane was in the air.

As before, the same two F-15's flew security with Captains Brown and Snow at their controls.

When Air Force two touched down in Hawaii, Jose and Dr. Tylor was there with a bus for the other passengers that were also onboard the 757 aircraft.

It didn't take long for the two-vehicle caravan to reach The Hope facility. As Professor Kovicha entered the building a round of applause filled the room.

Dr. Motto approached the Professor and shook his hand enthusiastically.

"It is a pleasure to see you again Professor Kovicha. Over half of us here were at your conference in Vienna three years ago. It was informative and helpful when researching genetic time lines and their development.

You just missed your fellow countryman Dr. Botanic. He returned to Austria for a seminar he has to give in Vienna." Dr. Motto said.

"Yes, I remember seeing you and many of the faces I see around the room. I recall talking to several of them."

"May I have your attention? I want you as a group to select one or two individuals to represent everything that Project Discover has found. They will work with Professor Kovicha and re-evaluate every piece of data we have gathered.

Everyone else will take a break from working on Project Discover. You will do nothing until your representatives and Professor Kovicha come to a final decision on Project Discover's final position.

Then, it will be determined on how we proceed. Appoint your spokesperson or persons to represent all of your hard work over the many weeks you have spent on Project Discover." Dr. Tylor said.

Dr. Tylor and Professor Kovicha went to Dr. Tylor's office to talk and wait for who would be appointed.

It took only ten minutes before Dr's Motto and Jones entered the office.

"I could have guessed that it would be the two of you. No one knows as much as you on the overall theories and findings of the project.

What you don't know is that this situation has reached a critical moment and time is on the verge of condemning us forever. In other words, the President needs an answer as fast as you can.

Professor, this is Dr's Jones and Motto. I suggest you three get to work immediately. Either agree or disagree on the findings." Dr. Tylor suggested.

With a stack of folders in hand, the three entered a small conference room and locked the door behind them.

"President Black filled me in on what was at stake. I'm impressed that you recreated the super cell. Dealing with any mutation can be an endless journey to the gates of hell.

I'm not going to review that process because it's insignificant now. The first thing we most do is for us to go over the crossover from the Goracks to our surface species.

I want to meet the Gorack people after our work is done here. I would like to gather some blood, skin and hair samples for my research.

Dr. Jones, please explain your theory on how the crossover happened and back up your facts to support that conclusion." Professor Kovicha said.

That was the beginning of a long tedious brainstorming session with monumental in-depth discussions.

WASHINGTON D C

Dr. Thomas Elvan, head of the Species Migration Patterns, was traveling to the areas that had been infected. He talked with Eric Tome of the Coast Guard in Alaska to get a report on whale activity.

He flew to Sydney Australia and talked to Dr. Shaw to see if anymore jellyfish or sharks were showing any signs of growth or behavior.

He stopped in Ecuador and met with Dr. Trevor Little. He was the man Dr. Botanic left in charge to monitor the Komodo's in his absence.

Dr. Elvan was thrilled that there were no reports of any odd behavior of any of the species that had been infected. The only major concern that he had was that migration patterns of birds and animals, from elephants to salmon, had gone astray.

The theory was that the earthquakes and volcano eruptions had changed the earths magnetic signature. That was confusing their inner homing detection they needed to return to their proper place.

Dr. Elvan left Ecuador in route to Rio de Janeiro for a conference on that exact occurrence.

THE HOPE

-------------25

It took three days before Professor Kovicha and Dr.'s Motto and jones came to a final decision after evaluating all the data.

They notified Dr. Tylor they had reached an agreement and he called for everyone to come hear their decision.

The room was filled with anticipation of what the final conclusion would be.

"Ladies and gentlemen, I will let Professor Kovicha reveal his findings," Dr. Tylor said.

"Good afternoon doctors and staff. After working with these two intelligent people, we have come to a definitive conclusion.

I will start from the beginning, even though you have heard and discovered it before.

The Gorack people for hundreds, if not thousands of years have been mutating their DNA and slowly developing the super cell. Every time they released their dead into the river, they were polluting the waters underground.

To a smaller degree, the lava consisted of elements that are in the super cell's DNA and contributes to its double helix. Oil also has properties that are found in the breakdown of the super cell's constructor.

Every time the hundreds of steam vents, lava vents and gallons of oil seepage occurs, they were changing the environment. The particles were released and the point of acceptability was obtained when they started to bond together.

As they grew larger, they were consumed by varies methods. They were eaten by small fish and they were then eaten by sharks. Same as the plankton being consumed by whales.

One thing we can't figure out is why only those four species were affected. It's our conclusion that the Goracks were the beginning of the mutated cells and that's how it came to the surface.

The earth is undergoing several catastrophic events that may be earth's Armageddon.

I was told that the Goracks used to control the earthquakes and Volcanic eruptions. They have been earth's guardians for hundreds of years.

When they came to the surface, it was many days after Kilauea started its recent massive eruption. After their arrival on the surface, the events started happening all over the globe.

I'm told that Rodic stated that the Goracks controlled the earths inner pressure. He believes that his people have been keeping earth safe by diverting pressure so it can't build up to a dangerous level.

Dr. Jones said that the Goracks are growing in their weight and height. The acceptable theory is that the ultraviolet rays and gamma rays cause a reaction on the super cells to grow.

After our talks and evaluating the facts, we believe all I've said to be 100 percent correct.

With that being said, the only way to solve the earths dilemma is for the Gorack's to return underground. They have to reinstate their abilities to control the earths pressure.

This is a two-fold emergency. The sky is darkening more every day. The air is filled with ash and smoke. It will become unbreathable in a week or so.

The Goracks are going to grow too big to return to inner earth by the lava tube. They must return immediately. They are the only ones that can save the world and that's only if they can do what Rodic said they could.

Are there any questions or statements that need explored further?" Professor Kovicha asked.

"Professor, what about Project Discover and all of us?" Dr. Zurich asked.

"I'll answer that Professor. I talked with President Black yesterday about this exact situation. The Hope as of this moment is shut down and will be dismantled.

The same is true for The Cell. Tomorrow Air Force Two will return everyone to their labs. You may gather your belongings and return to what you were involved with before Project Deliver.

The President thanks you for your hard work and dedication to America. Personnel from the CDC will also board the plane and they will be taken to Atlanta.

I too want to thank you all as well. I'm sure we will meet again. Professor Kovicha and I have to leave in an hour for Oregon. We have to explain what is needed of the Goracks and speak to Rodic.

Dr. Motto, it just occurred to me that you have the friendliest relationship with Rodic and the Gorack people. Would you like to come with me and help talk with Rodic? I can't make you; you have been relieved of any participation in Project Discover.

However, I'm inviting you as a friend," Dr. Tylor said.

"You know John that I would never say no. I'm on board for whatever you need for me to do."

"Thanks Lance, we're leaving in 20 minutes for the base. I'll make a call to the base and inform them I need the services of another F-15. I know there's several jets there for the Air show next week."

They soon left and arrived at the base. Captains Brown, Snow and another pilot we're ready with jets fueled.

This was the first time that Professor Kovicha had flown in a F-15. He had to go through the helmet and wraparound sunglasses before taking off.

In a few minutes the three jets were streaking across the sky eastward.

KLAMATH FALLS, OREGON

It was mid afternoon when the three F-15's arrived and taxied to their designated secured area at Kingsley Field. Dr. Tylor had made the right calls for their midair refueling and having Captain Anders and Deputy Looms meet them.

After introducing Professor Kovicha to the law enforcement men, they were in route to meet the Goracks.

Captain Anders had radioed Rodic that he and the others were coming to visit him. That was fine with Rodic, he figured it was just more of the same visits.

The two patrol cars pulled up in front of the homestead and everyone exited except Captain Anders and Deputy Looms. They both waved to Rodic, made a U-turn and returned to Klamath Falls.

"Glad to see you again Rodic. This is Professor Kovicha. He would like a conversation with you and the Gorack council. Dr. Motto and I have worked with him and we agree with his analysis of earth's predicament and the Gorack's future.

The leaders of the Goracks and you as their spokesman and the leader that presides over the council meetings, have to hear what he has to say." Dr. Tylor said.

"That sounds like you have something to say that's very important. Should I be worried? Are the Gorack people in danger?" Rodic asked.

"Yes, Rodic, it's a matter of life or death and time is of the essence."

"Okay Dr. Tylor. I will call for a meeting immediately if you want?"

"That would be perfect Rodic, you and your people need to know the facts sooner than later,"

Rodic rang the gathering bell and the Gorack's assembled in the center of the homestead.

"I'm Professor Kovicha and I have been working with Dr. Motto and Dr Jones for several days. We have concluded what all the data and hundreds of hours of research means.

I won't waste your time talking about cells, DNA, blood and all the scientific ingredients that made it possible for us to solve the many answers we needed.

I will cut to the chase and give you the bottom line on why I'm here.

The earth is attacking itself and slowly killing our planet. I was informed that the Goracks had been controlling the earth's inner pressure for hundreds of years. All this turmoil with volcanic eruptions and earthquakes started when you came to the surface.

I believe that by the timing and what Dr. Motto shared with me, about your home beneath the surface. I know that Rodic and the Gorack people are growing in weight and becoming taller.

I understand that Rodic asked Dr. Jones why he was becoming larger. I have the answer for you Rodic and for every Gorack. It's the sunlight. The reason is because it has Ultraviolet Rays and Gamma Rays in it. Those rays are reacting with your cellular development.

As the Project Recover members have told you, the four surface species that were growing, just like the Goracks are experiencing now. Those four species hearts exploded because it couldn't keep up with the blood flow that the body needed.

The same will happen to the Gorack people if you don't return beneath the soil again.

Not only would you be saving your race, by controlling the earth's pressure again you can save the earth from itself. That's a win, win solution.

I was also told that half of you want to return underground and the other half wants to stay on the surface. I'm sorry to say that all of the Goracks must return or you will surly die here on the surface.

The highest people in the United States government have discussed options for the best outcome for not only the Goracks, but for the surface people too.

We heard about Follower Trerd's solution in determining the Gorack's future.

When your council meets after we leave here today, please consider this suggestion along with whatever you may be considering.

After the Goracks return to their previous home. The government will supply you with any pipes, valves or gauges you need to regain your abilities to control the earth's pressure.

You will have as many ATV's you need to travel around and discover other lava tubes or whatever you want to use them for.

With the new coating material that NASA and MIT developed to reflect any temperature makes countless options available to you. We've approved a 12-inch pipe covered in that material to run from the surface to your underground home.

Inside the pipe will be electric, phone, cable wires, etc. MIT is working on making a flat screen tv, like the one you're watching now, that they can coat and make safe for use under those conditions of extreme heat.

Food will be delivered weekly to you, any thing you want. The President has authorized the Army Corp of Engineers to erect a building around the opening of the lava tube. The opening will be in the middle of the building.

The President is going to make the area a medical center for military personnel from Kingsley Field. It will also serve as a vet hospital for our veterans to receive the care they need.

If any Gorack gets sick, they will be brought up to the hospital here on the surface. A special room has been designed to accommodate the Goracks while on the surface.

The entire surface area will be fenced and will be a secured location. Guards at the gates at the only entrance will inspect and check on authorization before anyone will be allowed on the premises.

If for some unexpected reason that someone needs to come down to you, we have three suits at the moment. We can have more made if need be. We want the Goracks to have whatever they need, because you're protecting the earth and we need you as much as you need us. If the earth is destroyed, it may mean the Gorack people as well.

OH! One more thing, the government will give you a powerful poison solution that will kill the nutrient's that run ramped in the underground.

That's what I came here to say to you. It's up to the Gorack's to decide their own future. Does anyone have questions for any of us?" Professor Kovicha asked.

"Dr. Motto, is everything he said the truth, the whole truth?" Follower Jong asked.

"Unfortunately, every word of it is 100 percent correct. Sorry Jong."

"I've called Captain Anders and he's on his way. We're going to go back to Hawaii and await your decision. It's vital that you come to a final decision in two day or less,

You can see the sky is filled with ash and smoke. Most of the worlds people are inside their homes afraid to come outside.

If you choose to return, have a list of things you need to restart monitoring the earths pressure. I hope you do return for everyone's sake." Dr. Tylor said.

Captain Anders arrived and the three visitors entered the patrol car. The car pulled away leaving a trail of dust behind it. The occupants were silent as they traveled back to Kingsley Field.

The future of mankind was at the crossroads of survival or death and it was completely out of their hands to remedy the outcome.

_____26

CDC ATLANTA

As Dr. Zurich and Doctors Lintner and Stoner entered the CDC level 4 lab, the remaining staff members applauded.

"Welcome back doctors," Dr. Lamont said.

"Thank you, Dr. Lamont. It's good to be back. I guess you have all heard about the conclusions on Project Discover. Even though that project is officially closed down, I intend to keep searching for a way to kill the super cell, without harming its host." Dr. Zurich said.

"Dr. Motto will return tomorrow and join us." Dr Stoner announced.

The staff went back to the work that they were doing before the interruption. Teams consisting of two or three members were involved with Ebola, Marburg and Hantavirus. The CDC is one of the deadliest facilities in the world due to their research into these types of viruses.

THE CELL

When Captain Brown touched down at The Cell's secret location, it was raining in epic amounts. Dr. Jones entered the facility and went to her former office to collect her belongings.

She was startled when she saw Ben Wilson sitting in what had been her chair.

"Hey! She said loudly. What are you doing here Ben?" She asked.

"I talked with the President about the possibility of keeping this facility open and classify it as top secret. This location is miles closer to Washington D C and that would absolutely be a major benefit.

The President wants this facility to have the same mystique as Area 51. He wants to operate some clandestine projects and research from the east coast and not out west.

The lab and your research team will stay exactly as it is. New buildings will be constructed around this facility to accommodate other experiments. Your team will only have access to the lab by it's one and only door. The rest of the compound, departments and any other research areas will be off limits.

I've called a meeting for tomorrow at nine AM with your team. You can talk to them and let me know your decision no later than two PM.

Do you have any questions Dr. Jones?"

"No, that sounds like a great idea to me. I can almost say that 100 percent of my staff will love the idea as well."

Next morning Dr. Jones met with the staff of The Cell. She went over the President's proposal that he was offering to them. Their response was an overwhelming and cheering acceptance.

It was a good feeling for the staff to know they still had a secured government job.

THE GORACKS

After Professor Kovicha and Doctors Tylor and Motto had left, Rodic called for the men that made up their laws to assemble at the log clearing for an emergency meeting.

They walked with Rodic into the forest and sat down on the same logs that Rodic and Dr. Jones has sat on earlier.

They discussed the issues, facts, options and desires for the Gorack people. Hour after hour the conversation continued. To some it was not even a question as to returning back underground.

A couple thought it was all a lie to get rid of them. It may seem like an open and shut case as far as what needed to be done. But the Goracks were dealing with a situation they never had to face before. They had to trust individuals they knew nothing about.

Were they friendly or an enemy in disguise? The Goracks had never been in a position of believing anyone other than themselves.

One member of the council believed that the food and drinks were tainted with something to make them grow. They argued through the night and into the late morning. They came to a resolution that Rodic could offer Dr. Tylor.

Rodic knew that it wouldn't be the answer Dr. Tylor or President Black wanted to hear. He called Bill Wilson and gave him the Gorack's decision. Rodic was correct, Mr. Wilson was upset to put it mildly.

"If that's your final decision I will relay it to the President and Dr. Tylor. Thank you for coming to your decision in a timely order. I'll get back to you when the President and his advisors discuss this disappointing decision."

WASHINGTON D C

Mr. Wilson walked over to the White House from his office at the State Department. He used that time to decide how to update the President on the Goracks decision. The main dilemma was how he would respond after President Black reacted to the negative news.

He reported to the Oval Office and was cleared by security to enter and meet with the President.

"Good afternoon Mr. President. Rodic contacted me and informed me of the Goracks decision. They accepted all the perks you offered them. The supplies they need to restore their ability to monitor and control the earths inner pressure.

The food being delivered weekly. They especially love the medical and health care that they will have. The ability to contact the surface at anytime and the plasma TV, their totally fascinated with that. They like the porta-potties being there with them and that they will be cleaned weekly.

There is only a couple of snags to contend with Mr. President. Rodic asked about why the heavy equipment was digging where they had buried five of their people. I explained that we had to exhume them and the soil within a twenty feet circle and ten feet deep for decontamination purposes.

I told him that every time a Gorack individual died, their body needed to be brought to the surface and we would appropriately dispose of it. He believes that the Goracks should continue with their lifelong tradition of handling their dead as their custom.

After a long explanation, he agreed to that arrangement. He weighed the facts from my argument and finally saw the reasoning behind such a practice. Basically Mr. President I expressed to him how the mutated cells would contaminate the soil and in time, the surface world would be infected.

The last thing is that Follower Trerd refuses to return to the Gorack's subterranean world. He wants to die here on the surface. He states that he is close to death already due to a sickness he had before arriving on the surface.

He wants to enjoy the stars, sky, trees and breath the clean air with what little time he has left. Rodic told me that the Gorack council gave their support for him to do that.

All I need to get the new construction started and for the Goracks to start returning home is your approval of the Gorack's decision."

"I see no reason to decline their decision. Give me an hour for the White House attorneys to add those two amendments to my Executive Order papers. Once they bring the document to me, I'll sign it and then you can notify the Army Corp of Engineers that this job assignment is number one top priority.

They have the plans already that I approved yesterday. Face it, Bill, we were going to do this one way or another. As President, I have to protect all of America's citizens.

Go get something to eat and I'll call you as soon as I sign the papers."

Bill exited the Oval Office and went to the nearest restaurant and ordered a meal.

He was just finishing his piece of pecan pie when his cell phone started vibrating.

"Hello"

"Bill, I've signed the document. Get the Gorack's ball rolling ASAP. I'll call Dr. Tylor and bring him up to speed."

"Yes sir, Mr. President, right away."

INSTITUTE OF OCEANOGRAPH

Dr. Tylor was straightening up his office at the institute when his phone rang.

"Hello." Dr Tylor said.

"Please hold for President Black," a woman's voice stated.

"Good afternoon Dr. Tylor. The plan for the Gorack development has been approved and I signed the Executive Order a minute ago. I don't know how your workload looks right now; but I would like to offer you the position of managing that construction project.

You know the people involved already. One Gorack won't be returning and you and he can be supportive of one another during the construction.

Major Thomas Lewis will be in charge of all personal with the Army Corp of Engineers.

Your basic job is to oversee the construction and make sure it's what the blueprints require. It's not that I don't trust the Major. I feel better knowing that the cement is the correct mixture and rebar is the correct strength. I want you to double check that bolts are the proper grade, so on and so on.

It's the venders I'm concerned with. I don't need another situation explaining hundred-dollar light bulbs or cement so far below specs that it's cracking in six-months.

You will have the managing title, but what you are truly doing is being my watchdog and doing me a favor. I'll give you a day to assess the offer. Give me a call before noon my time Dr. Tylor."

"Thank you, President Black. I'm honored to be even considered for the position. May I ask how long this assignment is for?"

"If everything goes well, I'm told in the range of nine-months to a year."

"I don't need extra time Mr. President. I will gladly accept your invitation to manager the Gorack construction project."

"Thank you, Dr. Tylor. There are several very nice living quarters being delivered on site as we speak. All this was set in motion a week ago in preparation for this project. As I told Bill Wilson, this was going to happen one way or the other, no matter what the Goracks decided."

"When would you like me to be on site Mr. President?"

"Anytime tomorrow will be fine. Major Lewis and his entire crew will be there tomorrow. Local venders are delivering supplies tomorrow afternoon.

You should see lumber, wiring, windows, tools and a food out building. There will be several cooks and a permanent kitchen.

The local Caterpillar dealer will deliver several pieces of heavy equipment in two days. Another local vender will bring forty porta-potties until the septic tanks are installed and the plumbing is up and running.

We have contracted with a few of the local gyms to have our people use their shower facilities. As you can see Dr. Tylor, we are out front of this by a long shot.

I'm going to call Major Lewis right now and let him know you're coming tomorrow. I want you two to get together and get to know one another. You both will be working closely with one another for several months.

The requirements for the supply's being used are with the blueprints that the Major has. Make sure the venders' deliveries are of the grade, rating or strength required.

That sums up everything I wanted to say to you Dr. Tylor. Anything you want to say or add?"

"No, Mr. President. I fully understand what you need from me. I will not disappoint you or regret your decision to offer me this position."

The President called Major Lewis and brought him up to speed. Then he leaned back in his chair and fell into a much-needed snooze.

KLAMATH FALLS, OREGON

Next day the Gorack homestead was a massive unscripted menagerie of people running amuck. Venders unloading materials and dropping off huge trash containers. Once the trucks that brought lumber were unloaded, construction on the kitchen started.

The Goracks were dumbfounded by everything. They didn't know what half the stuff being delivered was. They wound up being in the way more than anything, but they were tolerated by everyone.

A cheer sounded out over the compound by the Goracks when four large trucks pulled up with 16 more ATV's. They knew that they were going to be used for the trips back and forth from the underground and surface.

Dr. Tylor found Rodic and explained he needed to talk with the Goracks as soon as possible.

Rodic rang the gathering bell and the Goracks came and huddled around him.

"Hello again. I'm Dr. Tylor in case some of you may forgotten. There are trucks coming this afternoon to deliver food. At that time, you will load up your belongings for your journey back to your underground homes.

As you see, 16 new ATV's have been delivered for your use. Each one has a trailer that can be pulled behind them. They have been coated with the same heat resistant material as the three we have been using.

Two of Major Lewis's team and Follower Trerd will accompany you on your way down the lava tube. Once you arrive and you unload your belongings and food, I need you to give me a list of what you require to re-establish your ability to control the earths pressure.

Then Rodic will return with the three of us to the surface. We are going to hook four trailers up behind each of the four ATV's that's returning. After reaching the surface Follower Trerd will bring Rodic back.

I don't want to make it look like I can't wait to get rid of you, because that's not true. The earth is still undergoing violent earthquakes and volcanic eruptions. Time is running out to save the earth from becoming an ice age planet once the sun disappears."

"We understand your position of urgency, we can see the affects already from the darken sky. We will depart as soon as the food arrives, until then we'll start packing our belongings." Rodic said.

Major Lewis had a dozen of his men attach trailers to the ATV's and deliver one assembled vehicle to each tent of the Goracks.

It didn't take long for the Goracks to complete gathering their belongings. They only had what they carried through the lava tube.

Soon the trucks arrived with the food for the Goracks and the workers from the Army Corp of Engineers.

It was shocking at how fast the kitchen was constructed. The stoves and other appliances were installed and a big 500-gallon tank of gas was delivered. Within three hours the kitchen was operating and cooking dinner.

The Goracks finished loading the trailers with food. The MIT and NASA engineers had designed an ice chest that was coated with the same heat resistant material as the ATV's. The coolers were able to keep ice for five to six days before it completely melted. The food would stay cold and not bake from the extreme heat.

When the Goracks were ready to leave, Rodic went and informed Dr. Tylor they were ready to go.

Rodic and Follower Trerd lead the long line of ATV's into the opening of the lava tube. Bringing up the rear was Ken Tiplord, the most trusted member of Major Lewis's team.

He was a former Navy Seal and had led his own Special Forces team in the middle east. He felt weird wearing the bulky astronaut looking suit, but he adjusted to it after an hour or so.

Ken found their decent to the inner earth fascinating. He was in awe of seeing the colors of the soil change as the deeper they. He was contacting the surface every half hour. Major Lewis wanted to know that his men were adjusting to this assignment that was like none he'd ever seen before. The Major was glad to hear that Ken was actually enjoying himself the deeper he went.

Eventually they arrived at the Goracks homeland. Everyone started unloading the vehicles. Rodic showed Ken the areas that were used to control pressure by rerouting it.

They took measurements and made a list of how much pipe, valves, gauges and the proper sizes and the different material needed for the different articles.

Ken was relaying the list to the surface as he moved around the monitoring stations with Rodic.

The list grew to an impressive amount of materials needed to repair and install to reach the ability to get it up and running properly.

Money wasn't an issue. President Black had given the project a blank check and a top-level priority.

When Ken had finished with what was needed for the repairs, Rodic, Follower Trerd and Ken started back with twelve trailers in total being towed behind them.

Major Lewis called the venders he needed to supply the parts and read off the list of materials he wanted delivered ASAP.

Needless to say, the people of Klamath Falls were as happy as if they just won a billion-dollar lottery. The venders were the most excited, in a way, they had hit the lottery.

CDC ATLANTA

After a good night's sleep, Dr. Zurich entered the lab and started to transform a mid-sized room into a one-man lab. He was preparing his own little lab inside the CDC for himself.

He had gotten a call from Dr. Jones and was thrilled to hear that The Cell was going to stay operational.

-------------------27

He decided to include Erica in his research because of her specialties in the field. He got a little excited when Erica slipped and mentioned that The Cell was on the east coast.

As luck would have it, The Cell facility was going to have a facelift and wouldn't be completely functional for a month. That was great news for Doc. He immediately invited Dr. Jones to spend that time working with him at the CDC.

The next day she arrived in Atlanta and was met by Dr. Zurich. During the drive to the CDC facility, Doc explained his intentions of finding a way to kill the mutated cells. The real trick was that whatever that was, it wouldn't kill regular cells or the host if the host was infected.

Once at the CDC and Erica saw the lab. She and Dr. Zurich established priorities and how to begin their research.

The first step they decided was to attack the mutated cells double helix. The only thing that was significantly different from human cells. Were the two extra sugar and phosphate molecules on either side of the double helix. How could something that looked so minor, have such a powerful effect on a molecule?

The CDC team went about their work on projects that came from everywhere around the world. There were millions of people suffering from respiratory conditions and different bacteria and viral samples had to be identified.

Since sugar was a component of the double helix, Erica introduced the different medications that are used for people with diabetes. None of them made a reaction one way or the other.

Both Erica and Doc believed that sugar was something that was part of their goal. The fact that carbohydrates, alcohol, starches and obviously sugar, became sugar in the human body.

They then tried introducing more phosphates to see the reaction of the DH (double helix). That made the cells molecular structure unstable and destroyed the DH completely.

That wasn't the answer either because it attacked and killed everything, including the good molecules that were need in humans.

Both Erica and Doc didn't expect to solve the problem overnight or in a week or two. The failure was looked at as a positive because it showed what wouldn't work.

They quit for the day and agreed to come back the next day with new thoughts for a solution.

KLAMATH FALLS, OREGON

The compound was being erected faster than anyone imagined. Every structure had its foundation and walls completed. The crews were eating in the kitchen and the security fence was up and was now being wired so it could be electrified.

Rodic, Follower Trerd and Ken were transporting pipe, fittings and gauges down to the Goracks. The work to repair the pressure monitoring stations was coming along nicely.

After three weeks the Goracks had the ability once again to control the inner earths pressure. That was a blessing because the surface had almost slipped into total darkness. Rodic delivered the last trailer of pipes and parts for any repairs that might occur and stayed there.

Many of the residents from Klamath Falls were coming up to the compound for a look. They mostly got in the way and hindered the progress due to the one-way in and out.

Major Lewis contacted Captain Anders and asked him to stop the citizens from interfering with the compound's activities.

The decision was made that where the road turned off highway 97 to the compound, would now have a secured and guarded gate. The compound was elevated to an army base level where ID was mandatory to enter.

That solved the traffic jams and made life much better within the compound.

Out of respect, President Black named the compound Fort Rodic.

A month had past since the Goracks had resumed controlling the earths pressure. The earthquakes had ceased, except for Hawaii's volcano, all others had stopped erupting. The sky was still filled with Smokey overcast, but the sun managed peeked through once in a while.

The people on earth that had been looting, fighting, stealing gas, food and rioting were coming to their senses and returning to how things were before the crises.

Three months passed quickly before Fort Rodic was completed. It was a massive compound cut into the side of a forest covered mountain.

People could see it from the highway below. The only way someone could get closer to it was to be a hunter or hiker. Even then you were stopped at the electrified high fence that was as far as half a mile from the structures.

The venders were virtually the only outsiders allowed in. The food, porta-potty and emergency vehicles. Captain Anders came and went freely because he was considered Fort Rodic's honored citizen. He knew from the start the issues and he helped in every step way in the development from the Gorack's homestead.

Many of the worlds renowned scientist were given special passes to go down the lava tube for their research programs. Everything from soil to temperature studies.

NASA developed more suits with better innovations built into them. However, no one was allowed to venture more than a third of the way down the tube.

Believe it or not, very few knew that the Goracks existed. That was something that the government thought was better not revealing to the public.

Follower Trerd did pass away a few days after the completion of Fort Rodic. Rodic came up to the surface to perform the Gorack traditional farewell ceremony before the government took the body for disposal.

It was nice to see Rodic again. He had returned being whiter than white from being underground. He was happy to see what the Goracks once called their homestead had become.

Rodic knew that he could come to the surface anytime he desired. He did miss the doctors that had helped him and his people in the beginning. He made a decision that the first food delivery of every month he would come up to visit and take the food back.

That was a fantastic idea. That meant his surface friends could see him at that time.

After hearing that, Dr. Motto and Dr. Jones made a point of being there to meet Rodic as he exited the lava tube. It brought tears to Rodic eyes as he hugged the both of them.

Dr. Zurich wasn't thrilled about losing both of them from the CDC at the same time. Erica was leaving to go back to The Cell in a few days anyway. He understood the deep connection between them and Rodic.

The sky was blue again and the birds chirped loudly. Farmers were planting new crops and for the first time in a long time, it started to rain.

The Goracks saved Mother Earth and except for a few, no one will ever know.

It makes you wonder if we really are on the verge of such an event. Could such a devastating occurrence happen?

Dr. Jones and Dr. Zurich never have, thus far, found what they are searching for. They did expose that radiation affected all cellular structure and molecules.

Was the Japanese's nuclear reactor meltdown the straw that broke the evolutions back?

We are absorbing radiation from our sun, microwaves, cell phones and countless other means every day. I live in Oregon and the results of the Japanese's meltdown are washing up on the entire west coast's beaches.

The consensus is that it will be a virus or bacteria that will kill off the human race. They both live in a world that few can see or understand. I just wish I knew where we as a species are on that time table to destruction.

I wouldn't count on Doc and Erica discovering the antidote to save us all.

LARRY WADE LIVINGSTON

AUTHOR'S PERSPECTIVE

I'm seventy-two and I've seen what society has become during those seventy-two years. I have to think that baby-boomers are saddened by what has transpired in their lifetime's. That's my personal opinion. I don't pretend to be the spokesman for the baby boomers, each one has the right to express their view anyway they want.

In the fifty's you could leave your home's door unlocked and your car windows down without hardly a care. Today you'd be stupid to even think you could get away with that for one night.

I honestly believe that the fifties were the best time to live in America. I know! No cell phones, flat screens, computers and hundreds of great inventions. They all make our life easier for sure.

I'm referring to the morals, traditions and one's honor. A time you praised our service-men and women. I know there's a lot of good people still out there. However, it saddens me how many have no pride, tradition, loyalty, respect or love of country.

You can't trust the government because their liars and crooked as a corkscrew. Corporate institutions lie and put the dollar ahead of the people's health or well-being. They say it's cheaper to pay out lawsuits than recall or R and D a safe replacement.

We live in a time where certain people break the law and judges just let them go free. The government gives our hard-earned tax dollars away like candy to the law breakers. Don't forget how many people get social security that have not put one penny into it, but they don't even live in America.

Children today have issues that are devastating in earth's future. Mainly it's their attitude and language. I see five- and six-year old's in the supermarket using every cuss word you could ever hear. Little kids telling their parent to F-off or eat S***. The adults just cuss's back at the kid with the same vulgar language.

I saw a child, approximately six years old, misbehaving at the store awhile back. I told him he needed to stop and behave himself. He gave me the one finger salute and said I couldn't make him. He continued with "if I touched him his mom would sue me" and continued doing what he had been doing.

His mother was literally ten feet away and overheard the entire conversation. She stared at me, but never said a word. She then told her child that they were leaving now. The kid looked straight at me and gave me that grin you all know.

What happened to the American dream? I believe that it's dead and buried. Sorry to be the bearer of such negativity. I will explain my reasoning.

The rich keeps getting richer and the poor keeps getting poorer. The cost of owning a home is outrageous. Fewer and fewer can save enough money for the down payment required. Wages are going up some. But not as fast as living expenses, taxes, repairs, medical insurance to name a few. These stables of life are shooting up in cost faster than wages. In a short time, many jobs will become robotic and only a few high paying positions will be available. That leaves minimum wage level jobs for people to fight for.

More people coming to America and jobs becoming automated. The housing market will have to few listings to give everyone a home. Even if one could afford the cost, the shortfall of homes will drive up the price for the housing that will be available.

P C to me represents one of the most damaging philosophy's ever to be allowed to run amuck. The children today are treated as if they are a marshmallow and must be kept in a protective bubble.

You can't say anything that might make little Johnny sad. You can't spank little Jonny either or you could go to jail.

This protective child raising practice will make little Johnny a productive and loving adult. Yea, you bet it will, what a stupid concept to teach children that's life will be so easy.

I hope little Johnny remembers his safe and caring parental upbringing. When Nick is beating the crap out of him because he told Nick he wanted Nick's seat by the window.

P C has made children of the future think life is a fun for all and everything is happy, happy, happy. When they grow up and meet the real world, there're going to be shocked.

If you take the time to honestly compare todays men, women and kids to pre 1900 individuals. You would see these people of today couldn't last a week under what the Santa Fe Trail days had to offer the settlers.

I feel I must say this. The United States of America is the greatest country in world. I am blessed to have been born and raised here. I thank God every day for that blessing. I hate how the liberal politicians are trying so hard to turn America into a socialistic society.

I'm not going to go on and on about that, because a liberal can't talk about anything that's not the way they see it. So, I don't waste my time on them for that reason.

Let's change the subject for a minute. We all have dreams and they can be very powerful in different ways. A dream about an incident that happened fifty years ago, can bring a tear to your eyes. It can be sad or joyful moment, but whichever one it is, it takes control of your emotions and makes you cry.

I'm glad in a way that I probably want be alive in 10 or 15 years from now. I feel sorry for the youth of today. They will never know how great America truly was at her finest.

I admire President Trump for all his efforts in trying to return America to when it was at its finest. Without help from the people and replacing two-thirds of Congress, it won't ever happen. Once the baby boomers die off, America will be lost forever to socialism.

So, I say to all my fellow baby boomers, enjoy the time you have left and pray for your grandchildren's future. May God be with America and continue to offer his salvation.

LARRY WADE LIVINGSTON

CPSIA information can be obtained
at www.ICGtesting.com
Printed in the USA
BVHW031036181019
561476BV00006B/46/P

9 781796 065121